I0521361

Night to Dawn 40

Illustrators:
Marge Simon: pages 15, 41, 64, and 79
Richard H. Fay: page 50
Mariel Milan Cruz: page 68
Chris Friend: pages 30, 60, 86, and 90
Sandy DeLuca: front and back covers, and pages 6, 37, 69, and 91
Elizabeth Hattie Pierce-Collins: pages 3, 26, 56, and 96
Denny E. Marshall: pages 19 and 84

Night to Dawn No. 40, October, 2021, Copyright 2021 by Barbara Custer. All rights revert to individual author and artist after publication. ISSN # 1542-1430; ISBN: 978-1-937769-68-0
Night to Dawn is a semi-annual publication of fiction, poetry, artwork, articles, and review.
Orders, editorial, and queries: Barbara Custer, P. O. Box 643, Abington, PA 19001
Email: barbaracuster@hotmail.com or ntdsubmissions@gmail.com
PayPal orders: venus1021@juno.com.
Submissions: ntdsubmissions@gmail.com; Web: www.bloodredshadow.com

Pickings and Tidbits

Top of the balloon to you! ☺

We're coming off the corona apocalypse, and the scientists have deemed the COVID vaccines 95% effective. As of this printing, many stores, gyms, and public venues are reopening, with fewer restrictions. However, I'll always want to travel with hand sanitizer and find it hard to imagine food buffets in a post-COVID world. That said, life as we knew it is finally getting underway.

The same favorable outcome can't be said for the characters in *Night to Dawn 40*. In particular, Lee Clark Zumpe's "Worm-sacks and Dirt-backs." The story opens with a maze of dead, shambling people crowding a hospital, seeking relief from their pain. Zumpe's other three stories have grim endings and themes, too, as many horror and dark fantasy tales are wont to have. Ken Goldman's "Young Girls Are Coming to Ajo" starts with an ordinary situation and slowly twists its way to horror, with a vampire using a small lizard to do her bloodletting. Gerald Browning's "Giggling in the Dark" also has a grim theme, with the dead laughing as they feed on a human.

Richard H. Fay is back at *Night to Dawn 40* with poetry and some of his art. Look for his poetry in upcoming issues, too. Mariel Milan Cruz gives her photos an eerie look, and I've published one with Todd Hanks' "City of Rats." Mice have invaded my house, and the story left me wondering if a queen was producing all the mice within my walls. I slept with the lights on after editing, head burrowed inside my balloons. Sandy DeLuca did the front and back covers for this issue, along with interior art. Marge Simon sent four poems with illustrations. Denny E. Marshall, Elizabeth Hattie Pierce, and Chris Friend also have their illustrations here.

Keily Blair's internship has ended, and I may have an opening for another intern. She was an exemplary worker. I'm delighted to announce the release of Rod Marsden's *Dragon Queen*, the sequel to *50 Dragons*. Both books feature futuristic SF fantasy, but Marsden's "Made in England" lends horror to his writing. His main character's behavior changes for the worse after he buys a scalpel formerly used by a serial killer.

Dr. Roger Darvell and his wife confront a ghost in Margaret L. Carter's "Desk Specter." Darvell is one of my favorite characters. If you wish to read more tales featuring Dr. Darvell, check out Carter's *Child of Twilight* and *Dark Changeling*. Both books have been combined into a Kindle edition titled *Twilight's Changelings*, and I recommend reading.

Losing a child is tragic. But, in Hal Kempka's "Instinct," the main character's child returns to his mother, but not in a way she expects. The sequel to Linda Barrett's "Lianne" concludes with our narrator and Lianne conquering the evil Ian Hand. Rajeev Bhargava's "Crepuscular Fiend" features a young couple whose curiosity about a haunted house gets them into hot water. They escape the fiend who's after them, but their safety isn't guaranteed—quite.

Are vampires ever disgusted with themselves for craving blood? Marc Shapiro answers this question in "Even the Undead Get the Blues." I was delighted to read Christopher T. Dabrowski's "Phantom." In the end, the reader wonders if the main character is a child facing down a frightful ghost or merely an older man in the clutches of Alzheimer's. Either way, the story left me thinking. An award-winning short film was made in England based on "Phantom": https://www.facebook.com/phantomfilm. Link to trailer: https://www.youtube.com/watch?v=cJQBOFLE4N0

Along with each story, look for haunting poetry from Lee Clark Zumpe, Marge Simon, Matthew Wilson, Denny E. Marshall, Todd Hanks, Sravani Singampalli, and Richard Fay.

In other news, I've contracted with Lyn McConchie to publish her books, *Another Fire* and *Some Other Traveller*. The killer virus in these books makes COVID seem like the common cold. I'm continuing to plod along with my sequel to *When Blood Reigns*. My character Maddie has gotten more assertive, and I have a working ending at last. I'm looking now through the manuscript to ensure that everything in the story needs to be there. Author Kathryn Craft warns against theme dilution, where your book has a jumble of events, that while interesting, distracts the reader and writer from the central theme and character development. Killing my darlings has taken on a new meaning. While Grammarly is a great editing tool for work sent to NTD, using it on my draft has distracted me from addressing the cohesiveness issue. I use Grammarly on my blogs, and I recommend it as an editing tool for line edits and proofing.

I want to close with a big thank you to all the authors, poets, and illustrators who've sent me their work. And I want to thank the readers. I appreciate any attention given to my work.

~ *Barbara*

This Blasphemous Mockery
by
Lee Clark Zumpe

Joe recoiled from the sight of the subway every evening around 7:30 p.m. A tradition that had lasted eleven years, he had learned to detest his nightly ride beneath the streets of New York. The way the metal serpent slithered below the ground repulsed him. Some nights he spent the journey staring out the window, beyond his faint reflection. The thin membrane of concrete had worn so thin in a few places he could see the goings-on of Hell on the other side of the facade. A host of eager demons glared back at him.

All the disguises seemed to be deteriorating as the guillotine edge of the coming apocalypse drew closer. Sometimes he saw dark gods squirming in shadowy alleyways, taunting homeless drunkards. He heard wicked whispers billowing out of sewer drains, saw indescribable things shuffling across the rooftops of tenement buildings by night.

Long ago, he thought he might be losing his mind. Back then, he feared that these things he saw came only for him – that he alone was the target of their malfeasance. He sought professional help at the urging of his concerned wife, who promised him everything would work out. Stretched out on an uncomfortable sofa, Joe revealed his nightmares, recounted all those ghastly visions in a two-hour session with a psychotherapist.

By the close of the two hours, he was convinced the psychotherapist was one of them.

Shortly afterward, they took his wife away. The action did not surprise him, really. He saw her go. It appeared quite mundane to the uneducated onlooker: She seemed to leave willingly, arm wrapped about some tall fellow in an expensive three-piece suit. Joe knew better. He could see the man's tail curled up in his trousers. He could see facial tentacles writhing just below the artificial layer of flesh, and he could smell the demon's repugnant breath long after he had gone.

Who dares insult us with this blasphemous mockery, he had whispered to himself as the thing escorted her to some hellish condemnation.

Joe mourned Elizabeth's disappearance for months, even contemplated suicide. But in the end, he recognized his duty to society. Joe was one of the few that could see beyond the subterfuge. He realized that the demons had much larger objectives than torturing him: They had begun some kind of incursion, an invasion. He could not sit idly by and let them conquer New York City.

As the subway shuddered to a stop, Joe eyed the passengers around him. Expressionless toilers, innocent and ignorant, they milled about the car. He could see the wrinkles creeping along their flesh even now. He could see the gray hairs sprouting, the bones becoming brittle. Errant proteins tunneled through their gray matter. Their worries over money, relationships, religion, and life so consumed them that they could not see the horrors that faced them around every corner and down every corridor.

Unlike him, they were blind.

Joe waddled up the staircase, welcoming the embrace of a streetlamp. He found the sidewalk barren tonight, and he tried his best to avoid the island of shadows that huddled at the mouth of each alley. He clung to his briefcase and shuffled his feet over the cement, anxious to reach his comfortable apartment.

"Don't make a sound," the deep voice commanded, and Joe felt something cold and sharp grind into the small of his back. Hands (claws?) clamped onto his shoulders and dragged him away from the light, pulled him deeper into the shadows. "We'll make this real quick, real quiet, and real painless, okay?"

"Who," Joe began, but he knew the answer already.

"Just drop the briefcase and turn around real slow."

Joe did as he had been instructed. The briefcase splashed as it fell into a murky puddle. Had it rained today? The city's backstreets always seemed plagued by inexplicable tarns, watering holes for the rodent population.

Joe spun around, lifted his gaze, and stared into the face of the mugger. A young, white man wearing a trench coat swayed back and forth in front of him. The blade of his butterfly knife glimmered when the light of the distant streetlamp caught it.

"Now, I don't want to have to kill you, man," he said, eyes jumping around in his head. "Just gimme your wallet and your watch, and you can go on home."

Joe stared at his attacker for a moment before reacting. He saw the double row of jagged blood-stained teeth. He saw the black-on-black eyes that snapped shut sideways. He saw the thin viper tongue dancing in the deep chasm of its mouth.

In one swift, graceful move, Joe forced the blade from the demon's hand and broke its arm. Years of disciplined martial arts training offered him more security than any scripture ever had.

"Shit!" the demon said as tears bubbled to its eyes.

Joe dragged the demon, kicking and screaming, back into the belly of the alley. He kicked it in the chest several times, broke a few ribs, then threw it roughly to the ground between a couple of garbage cans. Its paws came up, waving, begging for mercy.

"Don't hurt me, man ... please," it pleaded.

Joe shrugged and stomped on its windpipe. Then he went to work. In a few minutes, the thing's facial tentacles were whipping about frantically, and a hundred eyes stared skyward from its true face. Now, everyone could recognize it for what it was.

Joe neatly wrapped a handkerchief around his prize, glanced up and down the alley, then started for home. He grabbed his briefcase from the puddle as he returned to the sidewalk.

Ten minutes later, Joe bolted the door of his apartment. His cat sped across the living room floor and brushed against his legs.

"Just a minute, Daisy," he said, tossing the briefcase down. He fiddled with the thermostat on his way down the hall, and the air conditioner whined.

He entered the bedroom and flipped a switch on the wall. An oscillating fan purred as light sent darkness scurrying. He removed the damp, crimson-tinged handkerchief from his pocket. At the foot of his bed was a chest freezer. He opened it and stared down at his prized collection of masks. He had collected so many trophies he would soon need to purchase a larger freezer.

The cat jumped up and sat on the rim, enjoying the cool air spilling out of the ice box. She sniffed the scent of blood on the air and hissed.

"It's okay, Daisy," Joe said. He tossed the kerchief and its contents onto the pile.

"Just another face in the crowd," he mumbled.

The End

Brown Jenkin by Lee Clark Zumpe

I heard something scurry across the floor, upstairs,
And shuddered in the bed where I lay, half-sleeping.
I thought of Brown Jenkin – the horror with rat-like hairs,
And that atrocious human face – up there, creeping ...
Edging up the steps, wading into the dark flood
My lantern caught it – perhaps no more than a mouse;
No: I saw that thing once suckled on devil's blood,
At that moment, I knew I had found the Witch-House.

Desk Specter
by
Margaret L. Carter

"I want to find out if I'm going crazy."

Dr. Roger Darvell scanned the new patient sitting—not lying, a largely obsolete custom—on the couch opposite his armchair. He'd positioned the chair so that the sunlight filtering through the window blinds wouldn't shine directly into his eyes. While it wouldn't harm him, it would cause discomfort he wanted to avoid. Liza McCall was a slender woman of medium height in her early thirties with sepia-toned skin, her chestnut hair coiled in a braided crown. Her clean scent and rose-pink aura confirmed her physical health, and he read perplexity but not fear in the emotion she projected. Vampiric extranormal senses streamlined the diagnostic process.

"We try to avoid that term. It's unscientific as well as counter-productive. Do you have some specific grounds for concern about your mental state?"

"I've started seeing a ghost." She shook her head, projecting more confusion than denial. "I tried to show it to my sister, and she didn't see what I saw, so I must be having hallucinations."

She flashed a smile. "But I don't feel any crazier than I did three weeks ago."

Keeping his disbelief in ghosts to himself for the moment, Roger said, "You spoke of *a* ghost. Only one?"

"So far." She shrugged. "Isn't one enough? Since I go to the same church as your partner, Dr. Loren, I mentioned it to her. She said it wouldn't be professional for her to counsel somebody she knows socially, so she recommended you. So here I am."

"Three weeks? Did the—appearances—start then?"

The patient nodded. "I just bought my first house and moved in a couple of months ago, but I didn't see the ghost until three weeks ago. The house is only, like, thirty years old, and I bought it from the original owners. I looked up obituaries under their name, and nobody died while they lived there except a grandfather, who died of heart trouble in a hospital. So it doesn't make sense for the house to be haunted."

Steepling his hands, he said in a carefully neutral tone, "You don't seem frightened."

"Well, I was startled the first time. I thought, you know, how did this strange woman get into my house? But when she vanished a couple of minutes later, I had to admit to myself I'd seen her appear out of thin air. She hasn't done anything scary or threatening, though."

"Can you think of something that happened around then to trigger the phenomenon?"

"I bought a Victorian rolltop desk from an estate sale. Every time the woman popped out of nowhere, it was when I was touching the desk." She twisted her fingers together in her lap. "I think I've got a haunted piece of furniture. Either that, or I'm losing my mind. I'd like to know which."

****

Seated on the living-room couch in Britt Loren's apartment that Friday evening, with his arm around her shoulders, luxuriating in her delicious fragrance, the glow of her aura, and the burnished golden-red of her hair in the lamplight, Roger asked, "Would you be interested in seeing a ghost?"

His lover and professional partner sat up straight, her eyes widening. "Since when have you decided ghosts exist?"

"I haven't. Ms. McCall, whom you referred to me, thinks she's haunted by one, but I still don't believe in the supernatural."

"Says the vampire."

He responded only with a wry smile, since they'd argued this point innumerable times. Britt knew as well as he did that vampires were not supernatural but members of another species.

"Given your interest in psi powers and the like, I knew you'd want to hear about her case, so I got her permission to discuss it with you." From a bottle on the coffee table, he poured a shot of brandy in each of two goblets and handed one to Britt. They'd just finished dinner, delivered from an upscale steak house, a full meal for her and a nearly rare filet mignon for him. As a vampire-human hybrid, he could digest that much solid food. He relished the anticipation of more vital nourishment, both blood and energy, in a passionate interlude with Britt a little later.

She took a sip from her glass and set it down. "I discouraged her from telling me much about it, so I'd love to hear it from you. What do you think about her ghost so far?"

"After one session? To begin with, she isn't fabricating it in a bid for attention. She believes in it herself." If the patient had lied, Roger would have instantly perceived her insincerity. "She displays self-awareness about how incredible the experience sounds. She definitely isn't schizophrenic or otherwise psychotic, and she's not on psychotropic drugs or any medication at all aside from nutritional supplements."

"This may sound like a silly question, but what makes her think it's a ghost? Does it walk through walls? Look semi-transparent?"

He drank from his own brandy glass while recalling the conversation with the patient. "According to her description, it looks like an ordinary woman with a cat. The first time, Ms. McCall initially mistook the—entity—for a real person, until the woman collapsed before her eyes. A rather alarming sight, to say the least. Then the image vanished into thin air, and on later occasions it appeared and reappeared the same way."

"Hmm. Could somebody be hoaxing her?"

"I considered that. I'm intrigued enough to want to witness this apparition for myself, and she agreed to let me come to her home in hopes that I might see the so-called ghost. Nobody else has yet. Would you like to join the expedition?"

"Do you need to ask?" Britt frowned in thought. "How many times has this alleged spirit appeared? And does it always perform identical actions?"

"On the first point, she didn't specify. She witnesses the apparition whenever she touches an antique desk she recently bought, so that seems to be the source of the phenomenon. As for the second question, yes. The entity goes through the same sequence every time."

"Then it might be something else rather than the actual spirit of a dead person."

"Not that I'd seriously consider that possibility anyway," he said. "Both of our churches teach that the dead move on to the afterlife. They don't linger on Earth making a nuisance of themselves." He was Catholic, she Episcopalian.

"But your afterlife includes Purgatory, and maybe Purgatory could involve remaining here to expiate some mistake or sin, couldn't it?"

He shrugged. "That wasn't included in the catechism I memorized in parochial school. You mentioned 'something else' rather than a true spirit. Such as?"

After another thoughtful sip of brandy, she said, "One theory of haunting suggests a hypothetical ghost could be nothing more than a psychic imprint on a location or object, endlessly repeating an image of a critical moment associated with strong emotion. Sort of like a recording."

She smiled as she sensed a spark of interest from him, through their telepathic and empathic bond. "Ah-hah! You're prepared to accept that, but not a full-fledged ghost."

"Why not? We know from personal experience that paranormal mental abilities exist, including clairvoyance. The power of intense emotion to leave an 'imprint' on the material world seems within the realm of possibility."

"Well, if you've made an appointment to visit Liza McCall's home, we'll find out soon enough. When is it scheduled for?"

"Tomorrow afternoon."

"Then we can't form any conclusions until then, can we? As Sherlock Holmes says, it's useless to speculate in advance of the data." After emptying her glass, she got to her feet and laced her fingers through his. "Now, are you ready for dessert?"

He stood, abandoning his own drink unfinished. "You know damn well I am." They headed for the bedroom.

****

The following afternoon, a brisk, sunny Saturday in October, the two of them drove to Ms. McCall's ranch-style house in a suburban development off Forest Drive on the fringe of Annapolis. They took Britt's car with her at the wheel, because Roger avoided driving in daylight whenever possible. The sun couldn't kill or even severely damage him, but the headaches and other heatstroke-like symptoms were bad enough. As she pulled up to the curb in the cul-de-sac at their destination, Britt said, "It'll be quite a letdown if we don't see anything and Liza's hallucinating after all."

Roger walked around to open the driver's door for her. Used to what she called his old-fashioned manners, she waited for him to do so.

"That would still leave us with an intriguing mystery," he said, "why an otherwise healthy woman who isn't on drugs would hallucinate."

They strode up a front walk flanked by a closely mown lawn sprinkled with newly fallen leaves. "Doesn't look very haunted, does it?" Britt remarked.

"Well, since she didn't identify the phantom as attached to the structure, we wouldn't expect it to."

Ms. McCall opened the door before he had a chance to ring the bell. "Thanks for coming. It's in here."

She led the way to a room off the downstairs hall, furnished as an office. The aroma of floral air freshener pervaded the house, masking the faint scent of cat litter. The cat itself, naturally, remained hidden, since most animals instinctively avoided vampires. Upon entering the office, Roger removed his sunglasses and scanned the area. A wide, utilitarian desk held a computer and printer, next to a bookcase stocked with reference works on architecture. On the opposite wall, beside the window, the allegedly haunted Victorian rolltop desk contrasted sharply with the file cabinet adjoining it as well as the contemporary design of the rest of the décor.

Britt ran a finger over the aged oak surface. Nothing happened, of course. "So this is the source of the problem. We've considered whether somebody might be playing a prank on you."

"Who'd go to that trouble, and why?" their hostess said. "They'd have to set it up to project a hologram or something whenever I touched the desk. If that's possible at all, it would be complicated and expensive, wouldn't it?"

Britt nodded. "Can't argue with that. Also, I'm not sure it is possible without equipment too obvious to hide."

"Plus, my sister would have to be in on it. Remember, the ghost appeared when she was here, and she said she didn't see it. She doesn't have any reason to gaslight me."

"Are you acquainted with anyone who does?" Roger asked.

The woman shook her head. "What would it get them? And I don't know anybody with a sense of so-called humor that twisted."

Britt touched the desktop again. "You said it appears whenever you make contact with the desk, right? Can you make it happen at will?"

"Yeah, and when I don't will it, too. It's not exactly scary, but I'd still like to be able to use a piece of furniture I paid over eight hundred dollars for, without getting a death scene shoved in my face every time."

Roger examined the offending object without touching it. Made of richly polished oak, it had a center drawer flanked by four small drawers on the left side and two small and one large, double-size drawer on the right. The rolltop cover was down, leaving a narrow strip of flat surface in front of it. "Can you demonstrate, please?" Roger folded his arms, leaning against the computer desk.

Ms. McCall rested the palm of her right hand on top of the antique piece. If anything were to happen, Roger expected it to be preceded by some otherworldly harbinger, such as an ethereal mist. Instead, the vision simply—appeared.

Carefully concealing his amazement behind a neutral stare, he silently asked Britt, *Do you see that? Nope, nothing.*

"There it is," their hostess whispered.

"Yes," Roger said. "You aren't delusional or hallucinating." It didn't surprise him that he perceived the apparition while Britt didn't. Tests over the years had revealed that she possessed no psi abilities of her own, only what she shared when Roger's mind touched hers. Ms. McCall, on the other hand, must be one of the rare human beings with a genuine gift, as opposed to the innumerable fraudulent claimants to such powers. He focused on his bond with Britt, allowing her to link with him and see through his eyes.

"Fascinating," he said. "Is it always silent?"

Ms. McCall nodded. "Like an old-time movie clip, but in color."

The "ghost" was a plump, middle-aged woman with salt-and-pepper hair in a tight bun. She wore an ankle-length, turquoise blue dress with a fitted waist and long sleeves. In her arms, she cradled a long-haired, tortoiseshell cat. Taking one unsteady step, she gasped and clutched her bosom, dropping the cat, which landed on the floor with its mouth open in a soundless yowl. The woman stumbled, groped for the edge of the desk, and crumpled to the floor. As she fell, she hit her head on the corner of the desk. She lay in a heap, face up, and didn't move again. With a silent meow, the cat kneaded her chest. After a few more seconds, the vision faded away.

"Amazing," Roger said. "I wonder whether we saw exactly the same thing." When she opened her mouth to answer, he held up a hand to stop her. "No, don't tell me. We'll each write down our impressions and compare them."

She dug into the larger desk, which held the computer, for two pads and pencils, and handed one to him. For the next couple of minutes, Roger jotted down the details of the apparition he'd witnessed, while she did the same. When they'd finished, he gave both sheets of paper to Britt. "Dr. Loren will deliver an unbiased verdict on whether our accounts agree."

After reading both, Britt said, "Except for minor differences in wording, the descriptions are identical."

Roger took the notes from her and placed them beside the computer. "I'd say that confirms the objective realty of the experience. Does the action ever vary in any way?"

Ms. McCall shook her head. "Exactly the same every time."

"Touching the surface invariably makes it appear? Does that mean if you do so right now, we'll witness the same phenomenon?"

"Well, not right away. We might have to wait five minutes or so. Once I got over being mind-boggled, I experimented with it some."

"Just as I thought," Britt said. "It's like a recording."

Their hostess frowned. "Say what?"

"A psychic recording, that is. A mental trace of a past action. Whenever somebody with extrasensory powers—like Roger and obviously you—touches it, it activates. I couldn't see anything because I don't have any such gift."

"Extrasensory powers? Me? Before all this started, I didn't believe they existed."

Roger ran his fingers over the wood. Nothing happened. "Apparently, it won't appear for anyone until the reset time has elapsed, so to speak. What we're suggesting is that this isn't the actual spirit of a dead woman. It's an automatic replay with no intelligence behind it."

"Not a real ghost, then." Ms. McCall radiated relief at this idea. "You said 'recording.' There's no way it could be a literal electronic video, is there?"

"I don't see how," Roger said, "but we may as well check to be thorough. May I move the desk?"

"Sure."

He pulled out the desk, and he and Britt examined it, feeling over the back and sides, opening and closing drawers, raising and lowering the rolltop cover, and reaching into pigeonholes. All the nooks and crannies were empty aside from the center drawer, which contained pens, paper clips, and other miscellaneous office supplies. As expected, they didn't find any apparatus that could account for the image. Besides, if it had an artificial source, everyone would see it. He restored the desk to its place against the wall.

With a sigh, their hostess slumped into the chair in front of the computer station. "So if I want to use it, I have to put up with the not-quite-ghost?"

Roger tapped the desktop, whereupon the vision restarted. Bemused, he swept a hand through the ethereal woman's midriff and watched the scenario play out identically as before. "You may have to resign yourself to that nuisance. At least we've demonstrated its harmlessness."

"On the bright side," Britt said, "you also know there's nothing wrong with your mind."

"Yeah, all I have to do is adjust my entire belief system on what's possible or impossible. No sweat."

Britt acknowledged the comment with a wry smile. "But maybe you aren't stuck with the haunting—only if it's attached to the desk itself."

Ms. McCall sat up straight. "Huh? What else could it be?"

"Something inside the desk."

"But you just saw that it's empty except for a few things I bought myself. No way could I believe I picked up a supernaturally infected ballpoint pen at the dollar store."

"There's one place we haven't searched." Britt crouched down and opened the drawer on the bottom right, the double-sized one. "I noticed the outside dimensions here are bigger than the inside. It's not unusual for these old desks to have false bottoms covering secret compartments. Nothing that would fool a thief for ten seconds, but a place for the owner to tuck away things she wants kept private." She groped around in the drawer. "Yep, here it is."

Peering over her shoulder into the formerly hidden space, Roger glimpsed an object with a metallic sheen. Britt plucked it out of its niche — an oval locket almost the size of an egg.

"Looks gold-plated," Roger said.

"Wow." Ms. McCall stood up and reached for the necklace. "I wonder how long this has been in there. The seller couldn't possibly have known about it." She took the locket from Britt and opened it, then showed the contents to the other two. One side contained a black-and-white photo of a younger version of the "ghost." In the other half, a lock of salt-and-pepper hair lay coiled alongside a tuft of black and brown fur.

"Here's the anchor for your apparition," Roger said. He ran his fingertips over the shiny surface. The vision replayed in the middle of the room.

"Problem solved," Britt said. "Without this in the drawer, you can use the desk anytime with no paranormal distractions."

"Thanks. I would never have thought of searching for a secret compartment." Their hostess spread out the necklace on the computer desk. "I'll have to return it to the seller, of course."

"I'm curious to hear what he or she has to say about the provenance of these antiques," Roger said.

"He," Ms. McCall answered. "It was a man clearing out his grandmother's place." She gazed at Roger with a slight frown, as if puzzled by his apparently irrelevant remark.

He stared into her eyes, snaring her attention. "It would be a good idea for me to come along with you when you return the locket." A subtle psychic nudge accompanied the words. Granted, he had no motive other than curiosity, but he did want to hear the end of the story.

"Yes," she murmured, defenseless against the mild compulsion. "I'll call you after I set up a meeting with him."

****

In the middle of the next day, Sunday, Roger drove to the address his temporary patient had provided, on the opposite side of the South River from Annapolis. Although Britt wasn't with him, they maintained a telepathic link so she wouldn't miss anything. He navigated the commercial strip of Route 2 into a rural area with lighter traffic, then followed the GPS directions down a two-lane side road past fields and woods. Along with the shade from overhanging trees, a gray sky with light drizzle made the trip less uncomfortable than it could have been.

When he reached his destination, a wooded waterfront lot with a sprawling, two-story house that displayed gables and a wraparound porch, he found Ms. McCall, in a jacket with a rain hood, standing next to her car at the foot of the long driveway. When he greeted her, she didn't ask why he wore sunglasses in such dreary weather, so he didn't have to concoct an excuse. His vampiric influence on her had come slightly unstuck, though, because she did ask, "Why did you come along, again?"

"Curiosity," he answered honestly. Then, with another gentle psychic shove, "You don't mind, do you?"

"Uh-uh, no problem," she murmured.

"You have the necklace?" He glanced at the oversize purse slung from her shoulder.

"Yeah, right here. It just finished its latest replay."

They strolled up to the porch, where a husky man of about forty with a short, blond beard opened the door to Roger's knock. "Hi, you must be Ms. McCall."

They shook hands. "And this is Dr. Darvell." She didn't explain Roger's presence, and the man didn't ask.

"I'm George Callahan. Come on in." The house had that echoey feeling unoccupied dwellings tended to take on. Traces of dust and mildew hovered in the air. He led the way through the entry hall into a room on the right, which had probably once been a parlor. Now its only furniture was a shabby couch next to the empty fireplace. "Sorry about the ambiance, or lack thereof. We're still trying to decide whether to sell. It's been in the family for generations." He waved them to the couch and sat at one end. "If that locket is what I think it is, I can't tell you how glad I am you found it."

Ms. McCall plucked the necklace out of her purse and dangled its chain between her fingers.

He took it from her and opened the locket, a smile of wonder spreading over his face. "Grandma showed me this when I was in high school, working on a family history assignment. I haven't seen it since. When it didn't turn up in her jewelry, we thought it was permanently lost. Where did you find it?"

Ms. McCall explained about the secret compartment.

"It's a family heirloom?" Roger asked. "Victorian, I'd guess?" He sensed Britt watching and listening through his mind.

"My grandmother inherited it from her grandmother." Mr. Callahan showed him the snapshot inside. "This is Grandma's great-grandmother. After she died, they saved a lock of her hair in the necklace, the way people often did in those days. As the story goes, she dropped dead of a heart attack when nobody was around except her cat, so they put some of the cat's fur in the locket, too." He glanced down for a second. "Pretty silly, huh?"

"I think it sounds kind of sweet," Ms. McCall said.

"Anyway, I'm grateful to have it back, and the rest of the family will be, too. Will you accept a reward?"

She emphatically shook her head. "I just did what any decent person would do. No trouble." She stood up.

Roger followed her cue. "We won't take up any more of your time, then."

When he shook their host's hand in farewell, he brushed against the chain of the necklace. The specters of the lady and cat materialized. Mr. Callahan, now shaking hands with Ms. McCall, was clearly oblivious to the apparition.

This time, though, it didn't reenact its death scene. Instead, the woman appeared to gaze straight into Roger's eyes. Her mouth soundlessly formed the words, "Thank you."

As the two of them strode down the driveway, Ms. McCall said to Roger, "Did you see that? Or am I really having hallucinations now?"

Stunned, he replied only, "Yes, I saw it."

So did I, Britt remarked inside his head. She radiated unmistakable satisfaction, verging on smugness. *Just a recording, right? After all, ghosts don't exist.*

The End

If you'd like to become better acquainted with Dr. Roger Darvell, he's introduced in Dark Changeling and Child of Twilight, which have been combined in a Kindle edition titled Twilight's Changelings: http://www.tinyurl.com/TwilightsChangelings. Please explore love among the monsters at Carter's Crypt: http://www.margaretlcarter.com. Also, Shadow of the Beast, the werewolf novel whose heroine is referenced in "Werewolf Watch," is finally back in print, here:

http://www.writers-exchange.com/Shadow-of-the-Beast/

Young Witch by Marge Simon

She remembers me,
she and her familiar --
how she loves that cat,
loves the way his fangs
draw my blood
as she smiles
her wine sweet smile,
lips tinged with poison.

With those dark eyes
she sees into forever,
conjures craven dreams --
the kind that men
mistake for lust,
and soon enough
she'll add another skull
to match my own;
inside she'll stick
another wick and light
her odious candle.

Hate of Dead Places by Matthew Wilson

Urns of dead queens' ashes
rattled by curious treasure hunters
looking for treasure therein
disturbed by scorched stake inside.

An Unfaithful Wife by Matthew Wilson

As the king's executioner, I raised my blade for good
There is no great action without great sin
I killed his wolfen queen and was soaked with blood
Glad of my payment till the moon will rip my skin.

Made in England
by
Rod Marsden

There are truly strange hobbies and collections. Thomas Renton had the strangest of all. He collected vintage medical supplies, including books on anatomy and surgical instruments. He went to fairs and auctions. Occasionally, something would turn up at a garage sale.

So what was his interest in such items? He was a doctor who was fascinated by how medicine had advanced from the 19th century to the present. There was the human body and what could be done when things went wrong, questions of what repairs were possible in certain time periods, and the conclusions arrived at if the surgery went technically well, but the patient died. He felt that such a study, plus his collection, made him a better physician. He was not a surgeon but a general practice doctor, but through his studies, understood other fields of medicine very well.

One day, at an auction house in Cheshire, England, Thomas Renton came upon a 19th-century scalpel. It was the type used on cadavers. He bought it for twenty pounds. No one else bid against him for it. The handle was wood, and the blade was silver-plated with a tiny stamp on it, indicating it was made for a London hospital in 1887.

It felt good in Thomas's hand as if it belonged there. The balance was perfect. It shone in the light from the lamp at his Cheshire hotel room. He was anxious to get it home and so caught the early morning train.

On the train trip, he wondered if it had ever carved up bodies delivered to places of learning by so-called Resurrectionists. Digging up the dead for profit was the Resurrectionist's trade, and it was once a thriving business. Students needed dead bodies to study, and there were folks willing to provide them for the right price. This was mentioned by Dickens in his *A Tale of Two Cities*. The trade had either ended or was coming to an end by the 1880s.

Much earlier in that century, recalled Thomas, Mary Shelley had written the ultimate novel about resurrection titled *Frankenstein*. Scientific study and morality didn't always get along, and Shelley had pointed this out to her public. It did not, however, stop scientific inquiry of a sinister nature from continuing.

Thomas took the scalpel from the train station to his flat in Camden, London. He placed it in a glass cabinet with the other surgical items he had accrued. In the glow of his lounge room lights, it shone beseechingly. Night was coming on, and something was telling him that there was special work to do.

After a cup of tea, he looked again at his new acquisition. He put his overcoat on as if to go out and wiped sweat from his brow. Why was he sweating? It was as if he was running a fever, but he didn't feel sick. He then took the scalpel out of the cabinet and held it gently before pocketing it. He had to board a train for Aldgate East, and from there, it would be a short walk to his destination.

On the short train journey, Thomas tried to clear his mind, but thoughts of the gleam in his newly acquired weapon persisted. *Weapon?* He asked himself. *It is an instrument of inquiry of the dead and nothing more. Where did the notion it was a weapon come from?*

Suddenly, he was walking down a street and marveling at how much it had changed over time. Visions of the 1890s came to him. Back then, it was a microcosm of sin and corruption with overflowing slums. Cancerous growths attacking society were everywhere, and his job back then was to cut them clean, to remove them as efficiently as possible from the body of London.

Now he observed that those women the past owner of the blade was concerned about were gone. Slums still overflowed but for different reasons. There were more high-rises to try to accommodate the overflow. Only one pub looked familiar to his 19th-century counterpart's eyes. He decided to have a Guinness there before he started his mission. The bartender was friendly, and the frothy, black, creamy alcohol went down well.

As Thomas sat and had his drink, there was talk going around that drinking hole that he agreed with and would normally do nothing about. Now he observed that the women who had been a menace back in the 1890s had been replaced by strange men with blades that were slashing anyone who didn't happen to look like them or think like them. They hated beer, pork pies, and dogs. They were the new filth that had to be extricated from society.

Thomas left the pub in a fever, knowing what he had to do next. It was thus the scalpel, with his help, terrorized the terrorists on a night made for terror. It smiled as it went to work on flesh and bone. Faces were cut up and noses removed. Thomas laughed at seeing those people he used to be frightened of cowering before him. The knives in their hands were forgotten as they became victims rather than victimizers. He laughed until he was exhausted from laughing. It felt good.

By dawn, the fever Thomas had felt was spent and he looked down at a scalpel meant for cadavers dripping red from what its present-day master considered to be the scum of his city. As it turned out, the blade's new master was not sexually motivated in his cutting as its previous host had been. Instead, he was fuelled by the moral outrage and fear he felt toward the unrepentant religious madmen of the modern world.

Thomas returned to his flat in Camden, London. He washed the blade, returned it to his place in this collection, and took off his clothes that had turned crimson and black, and then showered.

None of his neighbors reported him returning to his flat in a surprising state. They had been afraid that night to go out because of crazed religious nutters and so stayed indoors watching television, pretending their city was still a safe and sane place to live in. The police were nowhere to be seen.

Those Thomas and the blade had injured and those they had killed were attributed to religious fanatics turning on one another. Talk of a non-religious person doing some of that night's cutting were ignored by the authorities. The police would investigate that night's goings-on but, because of political correctness concerns for the religious nutters, they would be careful not to hurt anyone's feelings or cross too many culturally sensitive lines in their investigations. This Thomas and the blade knew would keep them safe.

There were, of cause, the blood-stained clothes to consider. What was he to do about them? Burying them in the communal backyard would not be a good idea. Putting them in the communal furnace and firing them up would also get him into trouble. Something might be left to incriminate him and records were kept as to who used the incinerator and when it was used.

He would have to travel into the country with the stained clothing in a backpack and then bury them in the woods. What he needed for future slashing and killing was an easy-to-wash, plastic-coated apron, the type used in morgues throughout the world. He should be able to purchase one online.

The knife was satisfied for a while. Then Thomas learned about a bombing in a major English city. Young people had gone to a pop concert and were blown up for some scatterbrained religious reason. This angered him.

I'll go there on my holidays, thought Thomas. *The culprit's dead, he was a suicide bomber, but surely, he left behind a mother, a father and possibly a few sisters and brothers.* Thomas would hunt them down, observe their daily habits, kidnap them, and kill them all slowly, one by one. He would make them pay for coming to his land and threatening its people. He would make it known that it was not right to indiscriminately kill the innocent for some blighted cause he did not understand.

Thus, he would thus find a better way to satisfy his shining partner in clearing away the human debris in his country. He might even send a piece of liver or perhaps a whole heart if it was small to a local newspaper office. Newspapers were so important back in the day when the blade first went on a killing spree. Perhaps he could send a fresh kidney to the BBC with on-air cooking instructions. It would be a brand-new Jack the Ripper special.

The End

Empty Sceneries by Sravani Singampalli

Everything is haunted here
In this place called as
The 'town of the dead.'
That man in grey shirt
Says that even Paracetamol and Aspirin
Tablets are no longer used here
Because people believe that ghosts
Are hidden in them.
Hearing all this I remember
How my mother used to warn me
Not to eat the papaya seeds
How she used to say
They'll grow into papaya trees
Inside my stomach.
Even today I say the same thing
To the little children
In my street.
I enjoy the queer notions
Things which take me to another world
Things which make me believe in aliens
Things which take away my breath
When I know
They are nothing
But just empty sceneries.

Haiku I by Denny E. Marshall

child didn't sleep well
monster in bedroom closet
had slumber party

©2013 Denny E. Marshall

19

Giggling in the Dark
by
Gerald Browning

Now…

Once upon a time, Culver's Bay was once called New Salem. When the Salem Witch Trials were in full swing, there was a faction of men, women, and children who fled Salem and founded New Salem. Most of those factions were called "witches." These few souls practiced a misunderstood art and were persecuted for it. For protection, the ground that founded New Salem happened to be atop a cluster of "ley lines." These were supposedly energy and spiritual locations that, some believe, attract some sort of preternatural energy. Over a century later, another Salem Witch Trial-like event occurred in New Salem. Which was why the name change was needed.

With the crime rate that rivaled Flint, Michigan and an overabundance of cases that can only be described as "strange," many believed that because Culver's Bay sat atop ley lines, the city was some sort of magnet for the paranormal. As such, downtown Culver's Bay was known for having many businesses such as fortune tellers, Tarot card readers, and even a few paranormal investigators or "ghost hunters."

Glenn Shan was a ghost hunter who heard about the disappearing kids over a month ago. With Marybelle Withers, his partner and best friend, they investigated the children and found out that the kids all had one thing in common…

They attended the same school.

As she moved through the foliage of the woods, she felt a familiar chill creep down her back. *Mom*, she thought. *What is going on?* She heard a breeze coupled with a rattle of leaves, but it sounded like someone … or some*thing* … was telling her to run.

And then she remembered.

****

Two days ago…

"How did you find out about this?"

"Just … watch!"

"But-but … I don't-"

"Just watch the damn video!"

The room went silent as the two film students watched the little girl as she played in the backyard. In the foreground, adults and children milled about at what looked to be a birthday party. The piñata was already broken. It swayed sadly in the slight breeze as the wrappers of its innards laid below it on the verdant grass. The adults wore bored expressions as the excited children climbed in and out of the massive bounce house.

No one paid attention to the little girl who petted the fluffy white dog in her arms.

"Glenn, if this is one of your bullshit stunts that you've staged-"

"Shut up, Mary!" His voice shocked her. Glenn never talked to her in that tone before. It must've shocked him, too. For a fleeting moment, he looked ashamed. "I'm sorry, Marybelle. I just … just need you to be patient, okay?"

The young woman ground her teeth together, suppressing her anger, and continued to watch the video.

"Keep your eye on the girl in the background. The birthday girl." They continued in silence and watched the birthday party. The little girl in the background continued to stare into the wooded area behind the yard, all the while petting her little fluffy dog. Her lips moved, but the camera couldn't pick up what she was saying. The camera panned the crowd, focusing on the people at the party and not the girl in the background.

Quickly, the camera panned over at a 40ish woman wearing a blouse and a pair of jeans. Glenn Shan turned up the volume on the computer screen and the phone connected to the hard drive via USB cable.

"Melody, can you come over here, sweetie? After all, it is *your* party." The camera returned to the girl in the distance. The lens zoomed as close to the girl as the camera would allow. The little girl smiled at her mom before she reached into the grass next to her, picked up a big kitchen knife, and deftly slit the small dog's throat, spraying her yellow dress with dark red. Screams filled the scene, and the camera jerked to the side. Shan paused the video, which froze onto the face of the little, bloodstained girl, a smile fixed onto her face.

"Glenn, what the fuck?" Marybelle jumped in her chair and looked at her best friend. They had been friends since freshman year at Culver's Bay University. They sat next to each other during the orientation session; both looked bored out of their minds. When they revealed to each other that they were aspiring film students, their friendship was solidified. "Is this some sort of found footage horror movie you've started on? Because if it is…" She paused and looked at the stilled frame. "It is damned impressive. It looks real."

"This isn't some stunt, Mary. This is real." He pushed his chair away from the computer terminal and stood up. The apartment was small but well furnished. It was messy, but Glenn knew where everything was. The only part of the apartment that looked clean and well-kept was the computer desk, with multiple monitors and the movie collection on the massive shelf next to the television. As soon as he could live off-campus, Glenn was hunting for a cheap place. Marybelle Withers still lived on campus, and every time he found an affordable listing, he would email the listing to her. He went to the refrigerator and pulled two bottles of beer out. Wordlessly, he gave her a bottle and popped the cap, and took a deep pull. "Do you remember the video production business I started last year?"

"You mean the business that you gave up on after a few months?" Marybelle was rewarded with a smile from Shen.

"Well, a few days ago, I got a message. I did a Bar Mitzvah a year ago, and the family recommended me to another couple. I didn't have the heart to say no to them."

"You mean you needed the money, but go on."

"Anyway, I went to the gig, and … well…" He pointed to the stilled image on the screen. "Anyway, two days ago, a cop appears at my apartment wanting to ask me questions about the event and to take a copy of my video. He didn't know I made a backup."

"Wow. That's some freaky shit." She shrugged her shoulders, "What does that have to do with me?"

"I called you over because I think we can do a segment on this."

"What? We are a paranormal investigation YouTube channel. What the hell does a little girl going crazy have to do with The Paranormalists?"

"I called a contact I have with the Culver's Bay *Gazette,* and he told me that Melody isn't the only kid who killed her pet in the last three years."

"What?"

"Over the past five months, six children have killed their animals. Roughly a week later, they have disappeared."

"Are you shitting me?"

"I've never liked that saying, but no, I am not." He took another swig from his bottle. "And in the last three months, the last four kids have had one thing in common."

"Insert dramatic pause here." Marybelle rolled her eyes. "Out with it, already."

"They are all students from Jefferson Elementary."

Withers perked up. "Tell me more, Velma!"

"I would like to see myself more as a Fred." He handed over a manila folder. "News clippings of the four kids. I've spent most of last night in the library looking at back issues of the *Gazette*."

She opened the folder and scanned through the clippings. "I don't see the 'paranormal' angle."

"Then you must not be reading the *Gazette*. These kids are disappearing, and their pattern ties with a series of child disappearances that have been going back a few years. They also coincide with the recent rash of murders that have been committed by kids who were kidnapped."

"So?"

"So … if you follow those recent killings, you will see that they all mimic vampire killings. The kids are tearing the throats out of their family members. Plus, these murders go all the way back to the Tooth Fairy slayings."

****

Now…

With some digging, not to mention pestering a few of the children, Shan and Withers learned that there was a negative stigma about the woods behind the school. The ones that led to the popular park right behind it. So rather than just wait until morning and set out to find clues like any ordinary pseudo-Scooby Doo detective gang, the duo decided to investigate by the eerie glow of their night vision lenses.

"Whose idea was it to search these grounds in the dark?" Marybelle complained a lot, but she was a damned good cameraman.

"Yours!" Shan laughed, which shook the Nikon hand camera like it was a found-footage horror film. The eerie green glow caused the world to shiver. The young filmmaker smiled in delight. This would look damned awesome when it is uploaded to their YouTube channel. Their last foray into the subway system tunnels yielded nothing but small, sad "towns" that the homeless people lived in. Glenn was glad they were in the wooded areas near the school and not those tunnels. He wasn't claustrophobic, but he did not want to venture down there again.

The single eye of the camera caught Marybelle Withers moving in and out of sight. One minute she was there, and the next, the woods swallowed her whole. The small but powerful microphone attached to the camera picked up her child-like laughter.

"Do you think we will find anything tonight?" Withers must've remembered the comments that they received from their last hunt. The viewers wanted more interaction between the two of them. They wanted to know about the hunters. Neither of them wanted to be filmed admitting their deepest, darkest secrets, but they had to tell the fans how they felt.

"I hope so for these kids' sakes. Three of the missing children have already been found. One just as recently as a few nights ago. The police are stymied by all of this. Some of the kids have been found … only to have torn the throats out of their other family members. The more information we can bring to the cops, the better."

Bullshit, Withers thought about Shan's sentiments. Marybelle knew that those words rang hollow. She knew that the most important thing on Glenn's mind wasn't helping the families or the cops. He was all about viewer subscribers and fan base. The amateur ghost hunter scanned the area with her night vision setting. She was more worried about the park safety patrol finding them. The school had already chased them off the school grounds for interviewing the children without their permission. She was sure that they would have communicated with the park safety patrol and the CBPD. If they were to get caught by the cops, their next video would be from behind bars.

They had entered the woods from the park side of the forest. What started as a nicely paved pathway slowly grew denser with foliage. The smooth pavement gave way to gravel and then dirt and loose rock. The closer they got to the school grounds, the thicker the forest became. What began with occasional nocturnal creatures scrambling for food and insects calling out into the darkness grew into less noise and … soon … silence.

"Do you notice that there are hardly any animal sounds?" Shan's voice grew fainter. He was moving farther away from her. "It's almost as if the animals know not to make any noise out here."

She knew he was doing that for the creepy effect, but she did not want to hear that. "How much longer before we get to the school? I'm starting to get freaked out."

Her friend's laughter grated on her nerves. "Getting scared?"

"No." Her reply was a bit too fast. "I just don't want to be out here any longer than I have to. Besides, we are here looking for paranormal phenomena. I just don't see why we have to go looking for kids who have gone crazy out in the middle of the damned woods."

"These kids disappeared and returned to kill and eat their families. It doesn't get more 'paranormal' than that, does it?" There was a pause. Withers' camera caught a faint glimpse of her partner moving ahead of her. "What do you think? 'Children of The Tooth Fairy.' Sounds like a creepy title of our next documentary, don't you think?"

A part of Marybelle cringed at the exploitative nature of the thought. How many lives were snuffed out? How many families were ruined? And all he could think about was a few more followers on Instagram or a couple of subscribers to their YouTube Channel. The amateur ghost hunter was about to reply with a curt comment, but the sound of children giggling made her blood run cold.

"Did you hear that?" Her voice was low; hopefully, he was able to hear it.

"Yeah. I thought it was just my imagination." Marybelle could hear the excitement in his voice.

"I think it's coming from the school playground."

More laughter. This time it sounded louder, caused the hunters to stop. "What the fuck is that? What kind of kid is out there this late?" Glenn asked.

"No one normal." Marybelle Withers heard her partner's footsteps crunch louder atop the leaves and brush. He was moving faster.

"Wait for me. Don't leave me out here alone."

"We *aren't* alone." His voice was fainter.

"Slow down!" Try as she might, she could not keep the tremor of fear from her voice. Withers picked up her pace and tried to keep up with her partner. The foliage thinned out as she got closer to the school. The childish giggles grew louder. She could make out at least four distinct voices. What kid would be out here in the middle of the night? Let alone four?

"Holy shit!" Glenn sounded shocked.

"What?"

"Damn, Mary, you gotta see this!"

Her heart smashed against her rib cage. What would she see? Her throat went dry and her palms grew even sweatier. Was this the opportunity that they were looking for? Marybelle had wondered if Glenn was really a believer. The two started The Paranormal Investigator's Channel while they were freshmen in college. Now, four years later, on the cusp of their graduation, their diligence may have finally paid off. She reached for her hip, where the Thermal Camera was clipped to her belt. She turned it on and heard the familiar hum of the viewer warming up. She scanned the area looking for phenomena but saw no presence. "Glenn, what do you see?"

Suddenly, the edge of the forest appeared. Just through some brush, and she would be at the school grounds. Marybelle Withers pushed through the branches and then appeared next to Glenn. He was looking at the playground set a few yards away from the building and saw…

Nothing.

"What the fuck, Glenn?" Her hopes fell to her feet. She looked at Glenn out of the corner of her eye and wondered again if he even believed in paranormal phenomenon. For years, they traveled to some of the creepiest places in the creepiest city in America and they found nothing. A blip on a meter here and a strange noise there, and that was all they could show for it. Yet, despite that, they managed to amass a small but loyal following. On many occasions, always off-camera, they talked about their beliefs, and Glenn managed to convince her of his sincerity in wanting to discover the paranormal. Yet, Withers wondered if he was using this as a gimmick to make money. He seemed too caught up in how much money they were making. At first, she wrote it off as a means to an end. They needed to fund their research. However, just in the past year, they made almost double what they normally did each year. With the slight uptick in paranormal phenomenon and the whole Gabriel Brimstone killing spree a few years ago, their viewers and subscribers have steadily increased.

Ever since Marybelle Withers' mother died, when she was seven, she was interested in the paranormal. Her dad would tell her that one day she would be able to see her again. But at ten years old, Marybelle saw her mother at the foot of her bed smiling down at her. And this happened a few times. She knew that phenomena existed beyond their natural world. She made it her mission to seek that out. What secrets they could hold!

Her heart stopped for just an instant when she stood next to her partner in paranormal investigating and stared at the playground. There was nothing there. Her heart dropped into her shoes.

"What the fuck, Glenn. There's nothing there!" Her camera was trained on the jungle gym.

"No! Don't you see it? Look at the swings!"

It took her a moment to realize what she was seeing. The swings were moving, but no one was sitting on them. Gasping, she aimed her thermal camera at the swings but saw no cold spots. There was nothing there. "It could have been a breeze."

"Not moving those swings that fast. Plus, they are *still* moving!"

She had to admit, that did look creepy. Withers opened her mouth to say something, but a distant giggle chilled her to her core.

It was a child's laugh.

"Did you hear that?" She couldn't tell if Shan's question was filled with fear, excitement, or both.

"What do you think it is?"

"I don't know, but I'm going to find out." Shan took off towards the laughter, deeper into the forest.

"Wait!" She gasped as fear gripped her throat. His footsteps receded amid the brush. "Dammit, Glenn!" Looking through the handheld video camera viewer, Withers looked at the world through the eerie green glow. The crunch of the leaves beneath her feet nearly drowned out the soft giggling of the invisible children ahead. "Glenn!" She continued to scream his name.

"Don't worry!" His voice seemed farther away than she'd thought. "I'm fine. Relax! We have found our proof. We're gonna be rich!"

A newfound sense of anger filled her. They were recording. The audience didn't need to know that Glenn Shan only cared about ratings and the profits. "Little bastard," she muttered beneath her breath.

"This is gonna be great!" His voice echoed back. "This is-" Before he could finish the thought, something cut him off in mid-sentence.

"Glenn? C'mon, Glenn! This isn't funny anymore. What the fuck is going on? Where are you?" More laughter greeted her. This time, it was closer. "Stop it!" Her voice grew shriller. Her heartbeat thudded faster. "Stop it!" The laughter was louder. Closer. "Stop it! Stop it! Stop it!" Her hands smashed against her ears. She fell to her knees and closed her eyes, squeezing the tears that seeped down her cheeks. She shivered as if a frost chilled her to her very bones.

Moments later, she pulled her hands from her ears and opened her eyes. The silence was oppressive. No insects or night creatures made a noise. She snapped her fingers just to make sure she wasn't going deaf. *What the hell is going on?* She struggled to keep her wits about her. "Glenn?" This time, her voice held pure terror. "Glenn?" She panned the camera a hundred and eighty degrees. She didn't see anything with the extra light provided by the night vision setting.

As she panned a little farther, she saw three young children standing in front of her. They seemed to appear. She heard no footsteps or any indication that someone was approaching. They all held the same expressionless gaze.

"What the fuck!" She recognized the faces of three of the missing children. "What is going on? How did you get here?"

In unison, as if rehearsed, they smiled. The eerie vision made her blood run cold. She stumbled backward, and the children advanced. And before she could think of how to react, they were upon her. She felt their teeth and fingers digging into her flesh. The agony caused her to scream. Her hands clawed around her to find something to fight them off, but her right hand only grabbed dirt. Her wails fell on deaf ears. She closed her eyes tight, knowing that if she could see what they were doing to her, she would lose her mind.

Tiny teeth tore into her arms and the side of her neck. Small fingers stabbed hard into her belly. The intense pain forced more screams from her throat. Her voice went raw as she felt a tiny finger press through her skin, reaching for her intestines.

"No! No! Oh, God, no!" She moaned as she felt her gore being forced from her stomach. Slowly, oh so slowly, her body grew weaker and the world grew dimmer. She could feel death approaching, and she sighed with relief. A small smile tugged at the corner of her lips as the pain dulled.

The last thought that she had was if these "children" were spirits or demons. She knew no ordinary human could be capable of doing such horrible acts. Her gaze drifted into the sky as everything went black.

Her last thought: *Mom?*

And standing in the distance, a lone figure cried softly in the darkness, mourning her daughter's fate.

The End

Instinct
by
Hal Kempka

Cora stood in the nursery doorway, rubbing her bulging belly and trembling with anticipation. She was a week overdue and was leaving for the hospital where her doctor would perform a C-section. Her baby must have sensed her anticipation as her belly rolled with movement.

The aroma from the freshly painted blue walls filled the air. While she felt sure it would be a boy, she'd stored two cans of pink in the garage as insurance. The increasing intensity and shortening intervals between labor pains told her it would not be long until she would become a mommy.

The baby's father disappeared shortly after their tryst the previous fall, and she was flying solo. It mattered little, however, that the bastard fled his responsibility. She'd been on her own for most of her life and was quite capable of raising the child alone.

Cora turned and started down the hallway. As she approached the stairs, a sharp pain stabbed at her belly. She doubled over and backed against the wall. Her legs buckled and a gush of wetness ran down her legs.

She glanced down at the pool of crimson. Her face flushed, and a cold sweat drenched her face and hair. After she took several measured breaths, the pain subsided.

She placed a hand against the wall for support and waddled toward the phone. Just as she dialed the last digit, Cora passed out. She awakened alone and strapped to a bed in a dimly lit hospital room. The aroma of sterile antiseptic hung in the air, sickening her.

Cora glanced around and panicked. The sterile white walls reminded her of the psych ward hospital county juvenile services had sent her to a decade earlier. They'd deemed her a threat to herself and others, though she was only venting her anger for being abandoned by her family and abused by the very foster parents they placed her with to be safe.

She tugged at the restraints on her hands and feet, craning her neck left and right.

"My baby! Where is my baby?" she screamed.

The attending nurse hurried into the room and pressed on her shoulders.

"That's okay, Cora, you're going to be fine," she said and promptly sedated her.

****

A week passed. The hospital staff weaned Cora off the sedation enough for the doctor to inform her that her baby had been stillborn.

"Cora," the doctor said, "while your gestation period was normal, the infant's development apparently ceased around the sixth month. There were complications, and there was nothing we could do."

Tears streamed down her cheeks; she shook her head. "That's not possible! I felt it move inside me when I went into labor. I even sang and talked to it."

She became nauseous and vomited, realizing she'd possibly interacted with a corpse in her belly. After calming down and finally accepting her loss, Cora told the nurses her baby would have been named Egan.

Upon her discharge, they gave her an elastic beaded bracelet with the baby's name stamped on the tiny blocks, an exact match to the one they placed on her baby's wrist. She wanted to see Eagan, but the doctors would not allow her. They did not tell her, for her own good, that the grossly deformed infant had been refrigerated in the hospital morgue, awaiting disposal. Before being discharged from the hospital, Cora arranged for a closed casket service in the hospital chapel and a burial at the local cemetery.

After returning home, Cora wallowed in depression for days. She spent nearly every waking moment sitting in the nursery, either gazing at the walls or standing over the crib. She would twirl the colorful bird mobile hanging overhead and stare down at the baby blue sheets and blanket. On several occasions, she awakened in the middle of the night. She bolted upright in bed, sure she heard a baby crying.

Her swollen breasts tormented her with a reminder of what would never be. When she tried pumping them, the unit's suction delivered milk mixed with crimson swirls of blood. After several days, her complexion turned sallow, and she lost weight.

Finally, her friend Maddy convinced her to get away for a while.

"Take some time for you, Cora. Go somewhere and relax. Gain a fresh perspective."

Cora reluctantly agreed but could not think of where to go. She remembered that her grandfather had built an old hunting cabin when she was a little girl, and her father told her about how secluded it was. Though she inherited the property after he died, she'd never been there; she'd forgotten entirely about it.

She dug through a box of miscellaneous family items and found the key and papers. Perhaps fresh air and seclusion might be what she needed. Since no one had been there in years, Cora hoped it hadn't been vandalized or destroyed.

While Cora dragged her luggage and supplies to her car, she noticed there were blood smears on her car door and side panel, as though someone was bleeding while they tried to break into her car. Either that or she hit something, though blood would have been on the front instead of the car's sides. She didn't remember hitting anything and figured that she probably was too preoccupied to realize it if she had hit something.

The following day, she left for the cabin. A few times during the drive along the narrow highway, a putrid odor like that of roadkill flowed through the air vents. It smelled like roadkill, and she ignored it the best she could. The seven-hour drive took its toll, and by the time she arrived, her eyes were puffy and gritty.

Cora felt relieved upon reaching the turnoff that led to the cabin. She followed the weeded-over, gravel road through a thick stand of gnarled oaks and pines that hovered overhead.

Her heart sank upon arriving. The cabin sat in a clearing with a picture-perfect view of the small lake. However, siding hung from the faded exterior walls, and the place looked to be in severe disrepair. It also appeared like critters had tried on numerous occasions to gnaw their way through the wood.

The rickety door stuck, and she pushed her shoulder against it. It opened into a great room, and the damp, musty odor of old rotting canvas cover hung heavy in the air. A thick layer of dust had settled on the sheets covering the furniture.

After unloading the car, Cora turned on the electricity and put her groceries away. Later, she walked down to the lake and sat on the boat dock. The gentle lap of waves against the shore and the eerie cry of a loon mesmerized her. She dangled her feet into the water and drank in the pastel, multi-hued sunset.

Cora succumbed to the solitude and felt her muscles relax. Minutes later, a strange sound that resembled a low, goatlike bleating startled her. She craned her neck and looked toward the shore. A shiver ran down her spine while she listened and scanned the thick stand of trees that lined the shore-line. She heard nothing more and wandered back to the cabin.

For the next few days, she cleaned and patched holes. Before long, freshening up the old place lessened her depression. Cora came to enjoy the solitude more and more.

Walks along the shore confirmed the seclusion, as she saw no other docks or houses, just thick stands of tall pines. She took the rowboat out onto the lake once or twice and dropped a fishing line into the water. It made no difference, though, as she didn't know how to fish and never caught anything.

One afternoon, she found an overgrown hiking path and followed it into the woods. As she breathed in the crisp pine scent, she again heard the faint but plaintive bleating, like that of a young goat.

Cora froze and the hair on her neck rose. It seemed odd as she did not remember seeing any farms or pastures. She listened for a few minutes, heard nothing more, and continued along the trail. Shafts of pale sunlight darted through the trees.

After hiking for almost an hour, Cora sat on an old log to rest. The pine scent gave way to a fetid odor. Something rustled in the underbrush. She sprang to her feet as a flock of large, black crows sprang from the thick bushes. They flew past in a black cloud and perched in the trees, cawing their displeasure at being interrupted.

Cora pushed her way through the underbrush, curious to see what they were scavenging. A branch sprang back and slapped against her cheek. Cora stumbled and stepped into a depression in the ground. She tumbled face-first onto a pile of leaves and twigs.

She glanced around at several small, rotting animal carcasses scattered about with the half-eaten remains of a goat. *That must have been what I had heard earlier*, she thought and stood. Something beneath the thick layer of dead grass and leaves grabbed her ankle. Cora screamed as a small withered hand with blackened, jagged nails dug into her skin. She yanked her leg, trying to break free, and fell into a thicket of wild raspberries. The thorns cut into her, and the more she tried to scramble free, the more entangled she became.

She gasped for breath and tried to scream but lay frozen in fear while a pair of shiny translucent eyes peered at her from the edge of the bush. A small creature skittered through the shadows of the brush and scrambled on top of her. It clawed at her clothes.

Cora squeezed her eyes shut and held her breath, certain she was about to be torn to shreds. Sharp teeth penetrated the flesh of her still-swollen breast, and she screamed in pain.

The creature bleated a guttural "Nongma" and nestled against her. She opened her eyes as it latched onto her nipple and areola and began to suckle.

All sense of reality faded as she simultaneously laughed and cried hysterically. She spotted something that had dug into the rotting flesh on its little bony arm. It was the blue beaded bracelet that matched hers. Her fear subsided while her maternal instincts kicked in. Cora draped her arms around the infant and nourished it as best she could.

The cries in the night, the blood on her car, and the bleating she heard in the woods shortly after arriving. *It all makes sense now,* she thought. Like an animal left behind by a family, instinct had led her little Eagan back to be in the arms of his loving mother.

He emitted a quiet and throaty growl, like that of a purr as she rocked him and sang, "Hush, little baby, don't you cry…"

The End

Worm-sacks and Dirt-backs
by
Lee Clark Zumpe

The sanitary world around Dr. Kenneth Sprague had rotted away, revealing its rancid underbelly.

"Who are we kidding? Reconstituted disinterred entities? The formerly expired? The prematurely lamented?" Sprague had used his last euphemism. Frustration and fatigue finally stripped him of his last ounce of professional prudence as he bickered with the chief of staff at Arnesville Regional Hospital. Surrounding the two men, the dead huddled in a once spotless hallway, many clustered in familial groups, whimpering and trembling. They had spilled into the corridors from an overcrowded and understaffed emergency room. Outside, they shambled through the parking lot, gazed despondently at their reflections in car windows, and picked at their own putrescent flesh. "They're walking corpses. How am I supposed to treat walking corpses?"

"Just do your job, Dr. Sprague." Dr. Zephram Ames responded to Sprague's outburst with a cold stare and an unsympathetic tone. The 50-something physician ran the hospital with an iron fist during the best of times. The current crisis had transformed him into a fascist despot devoid of compassion for his colleagues. "I expect you to treat each one like any other patient: Examine their symptoms, manage their pain, and monitor their progress. It's all that we can do until a treatment or a cure is developed."

"There won't be a treatment or a cure," Sprague said, his tone growing more insubordinate as his discontent and resentment mounted. Those who required and deserved legitimate health care were being turned away from the hospital because of the extraordinary circumstances. Sprague had not worked his way through medical school to spend the rest of his life dealing with an endless parade of moldering patients. "This isn't a disease. It's an aberration of nature."

"We have our orders." Ames referred to strict government directives outlined in a hastily drafted Presidential Executive Order shortly after the onset of the epidemic. "Our hands are tied. The law dictates our actions. I won't risk my career over this."

"And I won't waste mine medicating things that by all rights should be destroyed."

Sprague turned his back and walked down the grim corridor, navigating the ghastly tangle of fetid flesh and moaning cadavers. He longed for fresh air, untainted by the lurid stench of the dead. At the end of the hallway, he hesitated in front of a service entrance, wishing he could leave it all behind him, wishing he could ignore his conscience and go home and wait it out.

He could not help but feel beguiled by the bliss of seclusion, the promise of total tranquility as could only be achieved in complete isolation. At the same time, he feared what might become of the city – of the world – in his absence. What today manifested itself as a plague of the dead could tomorrow become a scourge of the living. He had an obligation to stay alert, to stay focused, to watch for signs of mutation.

After a moment's deliberation, he turned toward the stairwell and headed for the roof. Though he had no weather reports to notify him, he could tell a cold front was pushing through the mountains. He hoped the arctic winds would offer a temporary reprieve from the stomach-turning aroma saturating the hospital's lower levels.

Down there, everything smelled like the grave.

He had examined dozens of reconstituted disinterred entities over the last few weeks, poked and prodded them, even gathered specimens to be forwarded to the USAMRIID task force facility located on the outskirts of the city. He continually questioned the military's unprecedented utilization of civilian medical personnel to act as first responders in the outbreak, criticizing army scientists for distancing themselves from the hot zone.

Nothing about the epidemic made sense. The government's initial reaction had been to quarantine the city – a feat made feasible, thanks to the area's rugged topography. Set in the Appalachian Mountains in far western North Carolina, Arnesville could be cut off from the rest of the region relatively easily with the closure of four state highways and a 20-mile stretch of the Interstate system. State police simply rerouted traffic through nearby Canton and Waynesville.

A media blackout followed. All television, radio, and newspaper services terminated with swift and shocking efficiency. The military apparently deployed some form of equipment that jammed external radio signals and made satellite dishes ineffective. All phones, both landline and cellular, ceased to function. Postal deliveries were halted.

Not a single journalist entered the city after the implementation of the quarantine.

Then, instead of inserting troops to round up the infected corpses, the military positioned itself along the quarantine perimeter and set about patrolling the back country in Black Hawk choppers. No epidemiologists arrived to relieve the overtaxed medical community. No FEMA workers appeared to assess the conditions and provide logistical support. No government representatives visited to address the concerns of local residents, to offer reassurances or provide explanations and chart strategies.

Finally, word came down that the president had extended limited constitutional rights to those affected – and that the "killing" of any such entity constituted a federal offense punishable by, ironically, death.

Unlike those in Washington D.C., Sprague had no misconceptions about the state of the "corporeal undead," the term employed to describe the entities in the official document. The dead rarely spoke, exhibited no emotion other than chronic depression, and appeared to have only limited fine motor skills. He saw no spark of intelligence in their eyes, no flicker of remembrance, and no internal motivation to survive. Left to their own devices, they might well waste away into nothingness: They ate nothing, drank nothing and, aside from wandering and groaning, they did nothing.

Admittedly, some of Ames' closest associates had achieved some success with experimental therapy. His team worked in secrecy in the upper levels of the hospital, selecting trial candidates through a careful screening process. From the notes he had shared with other staff members, the things could be nourished intravenously, taught to perform simple skills, prompted into speech.

That Ames sanctioned such trials repulsed Sprague. Those responsible for the research argued that their work was a logical extension of their scientific background. They considered themselves medical revolutionaries exploring innovative rehabilitation techniques.

Sprague likened them to grave-robbers bent on harvesting the dead for their own selfish professional purposes.

"Fed up with the working conditions down there, Dr. Sprague?" Arriving on the roof, the physician found a congregation of expatriated interns smoking and sharing a bottle of Jack Daniels beneath the ruddy evening skies. "Or have you come to collect us and usher us back down to our stations?" Randy Donne had apparently been elected as the group's provisional spokesperson. The other greenhorns lacked the courage to voice their antipathy and aversion to dealing with the dead. "If that's the case, I'm afraid that we'll have to decline the invitation."

"No," Sprague said, "I'm here for some fresh air."

"Not much to go around." Donne flicked his cigarette butt over the side of the building, followed its descent with his gaze. The street in front of the hospital teemed with squirmy corpses. "There's so many of them now you can smell 'em all the way up here."

"Damn worm-sacks and dirt-backs," Freddie Julian said, downing a swig from the bottle. Sprague had heard both expressions in recent days, counted them among the more evocative inventions in an evolving lexicon. *Worm-sacks* referred to corpses over six months old, dug up by optimistic relatives and subsequently abandoned due to their advanced state of decomposition. *Dirt-backs* were the recent dead, in most cases spontaneously reawakened during their burial. "Someone should be corralling them, herding them toward a crematorium or something."

"That's not the will of the government," Sprague said with a hint of sarcasm. Black Hawks hovered over the distant horizon, combing the countryside. Occasional weapons fire had been heard over the last few days suggesting that some citizens had attempted escape. "For whatever reason, they want to keep them intact for the time being."

"Probably want to register them for November's general elections." Donne glanced at the stars emerging in the twilight between wispy bands of clouds. To the west, a line of storms crawled along the Appalachian crest. "Why do you think they've all come here, to the hospital? Why not go to their homes, their families?"

"They're suffering physical pain," Sprague answered. "That much we know. Assuming they retain some memories of life, they associate the hospital with feeling better."

"I guess we should be thankful they aren't flesh-eating zombies." Julian – not a particularly squeamish individual – visibly shuddered at the thought of how much worse things could be if the dead had awoken with a ravenous appetite. "I mean, that's what you expect the undead to do, right? Feast on the living?"

"I don't know what to expect them to do, Freddie." Sprague looked down upon the crowds, wondered how many had passed through the hospital doors previously on their way to the burial ground. How had the gardens of rest been transformed into the gardens of the restless? Julian's gratitude that they did not more closely resemble their cinematic representation led Sprague down another disquieting avenue of thought: With so many variables at work, so many mysteries as yet unanswered, no one could really be certain that they might not all rise up and start gorging themselves on the living. "Honestly, I don't think that they know what is expected of them, either."

****

The meat wagons began arriving the following day just after sunrise.

Dr. Sprague had spent the night on the roof with Donne and several other interns waiting for a squall line that regrettably stalled over the highlands. The first indication the day would be different came with the appearance of dozens of Chinooks sweeping in from the south flying low over the Pisgah National Forest. Like impatient buzzards, they circled the distant Arnesville International Airport, waiting for clearance.

"It's about time," Donne said, his upturned palm eclipsing the morning sun as he followed the helicopters' flight. He imagined the transport copters filled with anxious national guardsmen, ready to take all the dead into custody and convey them out of the city. Simultaneously, a column of black panel trucks maneuvered a maze of side streets and convened along Avery Boulevard.

Escorted by local police, the caravan carefully approached the hospital. Some shell-shocked residents stumbled from their homes along the thoroughfare to watch the grim procession. "Maybe they've come to their senses."

"Maybe," Sprague said, reserving judgment. "I'd better find Ames – see if I'm still employed." Before returning to the stairwell, the doctor peered over the ledge as paramilitary guardsmen escorted the first of the corpses into the backs of the meat wagons. The dead went willingly without any hint of resistance. They moved like cattle, without deliberation or reflection. "You all should get downstairs, see if you can help. When this mess is finally swept under the carpet, people will need our help again. That's why you're here. That's why you'll stay."

****

Sprague found Ames on the 10th floor. He had appropriated an entire wing for his team of researchers, ostensibly to investigate how best to treat the dead. Where uniformed security guards had restricted access yesterday, this morning Sprague found no obstacles.

"Dr. Ames," he called out, catching sight of the doctor down the hall. A tall, gaunt man with greasy hair and an expensive, tailored business suit conversed with Ames in front of a shadowed alcove at the far end of the corridor. From the man's emphatic gesticulations and boisterous tone, Sprague inferred a considerable degree of conceit. As the physician approached, Ames lifted a hand to curtail their tête-à-tête temporarily.

"Dr. Sprague, a pleasure to meet you," the man said, turning to face him. He contrived a disingenuous smile that unfolded across his pallid countenance like a serpent uncoiling itself to strike at some unwitting rodent. "I'm Bernard Chesterton, CEO of Therst Weber Pharmaceuticals." He began to extend his hand to cement the greeting but pulled back reflexively as if concerned about potential contagions. "I was just expressing my gratitude to Dr. Ames for his handling of this situation."

"I'm sorry," Sprague said, looking back and forth between the two men. "This just seems like an odd time to be hawking new drug treatment options, doesn't it, Dr. Ames?"

"Actually, Dr. Sprague, Mr. Chesterton is here to take guardianship of our corporeal undead. His company has taken full responsibility for the situation." Everyone knew Ames received kickbacks from the major pharmaceutical companies. His zealous support of their products resulted in endless perks and enabled him to build his palatial 5-bedroom mansion on a ridge overlooking the city while paying alimony to two ex-wives. In addition to pushing unessential prescriptions on patients through hospital staff and local doctors, Ames regularly advocated and approved clinical trials for dubious medications. "Because of its culpability, the company has made arrangements to oversee the re-education process."

"I beg your pardon?" Sprague needed no clarification. As he had suspected from the onset, someone behind the scenes had orchestrated the whole depraved enterprise – and Ames had played a pivotal role. The worm-sacks and dirt-backs had been intentionally revived. "So, you aren't going to destroy them? You're going to treat those things?"

"That's right, Dr. Sprague. It's no fault of theirs that they've been reanimated. Following a treatment regime developed and tested in part by Dr. Ames here, they will be reintegrated into society. Properly medicated, they'll continue to serve as active members of the community indefinitely."

"As what? Doorstops?"

"Come with us, Dr. Sprague," Ames said, placing a firm grasp on his shoulder as if to rein him in. "We were about to tour my makeshift recovery ward. I think you'll be surprised at the progress we've made."

Behind the guarded doors, air fresheners masked the stench of decomposing flesh. The revivified dead rested comfortably in hospital beds meant for the living. Unlike their kith and kin downstairs, these pampered examples had regained some semblance of color in their skin. They demonstrated a diverse range of palpable, though imperfect, expressions and displayed rudimentary emotions. Their arms and legs did not quiver and their fingers did not fidget. They exhibited a sense of purpose and identity.

"What have you done to them?" Sprague looked over the dead patients, flinching at their two-dimensional personalities, their deceptively sterilized appearance, their vacant stares. "You can pump them full of chemicals, but they'll never be the same – don't you see that? The spark is gone. Their time is already up. Science can't alter the processes of nature."

"Kenneth ... Sprague," a familiar voice called from out across the room. "Kenny, is ... that ... you?" Sprague went from bed to bed, searching for the speaker. He found him in the far corner, a copy of the Bible lying spread-eagle on his dinner tray. "It's ... good ... to see ... you ... Kenny."

"Uncle Howard?" Sprague's uncle had been dead for two years. The cancer that claimed him had resisted every form of treatment available at the time. Dozens of mourners had attended his funeral, watched as he was laid to rest in the mausoleum at Serenity Gardens. "This isn't possible."

"I ... can't ... explain." he said, his words punctuated by uncomfortably long gaps. Sprague stared at him wordlessly, studied the glowing flesh that should be withered and wasting away. The corners of his mouth twitched as he strained to smile. His fingers remained rigid, his arms fixed at his sides. His eyelids drooped but he never blinked. "How ... long?"

"Two years," Sprague answered, realizing instinctively what his uncle wanted to know. "It's been two years."

"Why ... am ... I ... here?" Each word, each movement had to be meticulously calculated and executed. Even with the treatment, the body processes lacked the fluid animation of life. They had degraded into clumsy mechanics, driven by an awkward automation mimicking vitality. "Why ... was ... I ... brought ... back?"

"I'm sorry, Uncle Howard," Sprague said, trying to repress both his grief and anger. "I don't know why." Sprague swallowed the heartache he had relinquished years earlier, reminding himself that the thing in the hospital bed could only be a shadow of the man he had known. "Those men can tell you why," he said, turning toward Ames and Chesterton. "Those men did this to you – to all of you."

Around the room, Ames' subjects exhibited a collective flash of recognition. Their medically-sustained solemnity deteriorated rapidly as the revelation gripped them. At once, all their misery and anguish and restiveness resurfaced. Something else emerged, too – an emotion thankfully absent until that critical epiphany washed over them. With newfound hatred, the corporeal undead struggled with the restraints confining them to their beds. They fought so violently that the adjacent skin tattered and turned a macabre shade of purple. Their glassy eyes bulged from their sockets.

Sprague recognized in their hostility a thirst for retribution, for justice and, maybe, for blood.

"Damn it, Sprague," Ames said, beckoning his private staff of assistants. Aides swarmed into the room, prepared to sedate the rebellious dead. Chesterton, savvy enough to appreciate a bad situation that might get even worse, quietly slipped out the door. "Get out of my ward, Sprague. Get out of my hospital."

Downstairs, lines of dead had formed in the corridors. They stretched through the emergency room, across the parking lot and down the sidewalk bordering Avery Boulevard. Troops crammed them into the backs of the black panel trucks which ferried them to the airport. There, more troops loaded them onto Chinooks. When filled, the helicopters lifted from the tarmac, heading east to some unknown destination.

Sprague, now unemployed, joined in the crowd of spectators watching the dead depart.

****

Later that evening, Sprague rested on his sofa nursing a bottle of imported Irish stout. Cable service had not yet been reestablished, but local television stations had begun broadcasting live reports from Arnesville that afternoon.

Officially, an unnamed pharmaceutical company had been to blame for the epidemic. An allegedly unsanctioned five-year study of a drug said to promote longevity had gone horribly wrong. Ten towns across North America had been affected, including Arnesville. Exposure rates which should have been limited to 10 percent of the population had exceeded 80 percent. Though the root cause had been determined, the catalyst that triggered the reanimation of the dead had yet to be discovered.

Government troops had begun overseeing an evacuation of all corporeal dead entities from the stricken municipalities. Remote camps had been established to help treat and reintegrate the victims back into society.

At 8:00 p.m., the president addressed both houses of Congress. Sprague, on the verge of sleep, roused himself to watch the historic broadcast.

"Everything," the president said, "Will be … all right." Sprague sat up and perched on the edge of the cushion. He upset the bottle as he hunted for the remote control. "My friends at FEMA … are working with … the military," he continued. His speeches had always suffered from his sluggish tone and staggered delivery. Tonight, though, Sprague paid closer attention to his cadence and inflection. "We welcome … these people … with open arms," he said, his eyes oddly unblinking. His rosy cheeks seemed too red, like someone might have applied blush just before he went on the air. "And I … am willing … to ask my colleagues … in Congress," he stammered. His hands rested on the sides of the podium, completely motionless. "To grant full citizenship … to the victims … in return for … five years of … service to our country … in the United States Armed Forces."

The camera panned across the floor of Congress. Representatives and Senators applauded with mechanical synchronicity, their expressions lacking any emotional subtext. Sprague spilled onto the floor, crawled over to the screen as he scanned the audience. Though some of the older members seemed a bit disheveled, most projected at least the semblance of life. A few, though, had only just begun the treatment. Their ashen faces, their sunken eyes, their leathery flesh betrayed their lingering putrescence. Tonight, the dead governed the living. Tomorrow, the world would know no better.

Regardless of the morning's setback, unflustered by potential impediments, Bernard Chesterton, CEO of Therst Weber Pharmaceuticals, stood among the powerbrokers, contented with his coup.

The End

Parts Required by Matthew Wilson

Fellow with sharp brain wanted
must have good arms and legs
no immediate kin a bonus
contact Baron Frankenstein for details.

Even the Undead Get the Blues
by
Marc Shapiro

Alyssa's eyes snapped open like a gunshot.

They were the only speck of contrast in a terminally dark room. Outside, it was all the same, all black. Foggy mist seeping through the treetops. Dim outlines of rocks and debris. By any stretch, this was truly the end of the world. Alyssa had lived here for longer than she could count and continued to count.

Alyssa was more than 200 years old. She had been undead for seemingly forever.

She got out of her comfy bed and moved to her coffee maker and hit the "on" switch. When you're undead, you don't need stimulation, but Alyssa had over the years grown accustomed to the steaming aroma and taste of black coffee. She moved to a couch and sat contemplating the night. The last thing she wanted to do was go out. But after all this time, Alyssa certainly knew the score.

The desire for blood had been engrained in her soul since a long time ago. The vagaries of her turning were smoky in her brain. She remembered a dark night, a dimly lit bar, a mysterious stranger. She remembered that there was a war on, the Russians and the French, and that she was a double agent for both sides. But that night, the only business she was looking for was a good time. Things got bleary at that point. She awoke alone in a dark alley, disheveled and with two bleeding fang marks on her neck.

Alyssa had been turned.

Through trial and error and a few close calls, Alyssa had, over the years, gotten up to speed on being a vampire. She needed blood from the living. She could only go out at night. If she followed the rules, she would live forever.

Alyssa took another sip of her coffee. All she wanted this night was to stay in, maybe watch some bad television, read a book, or just stare out into the night. But the last time she checked, the blood bank didn't deliver. Alyssa took another sip as she cursed her fate.

Alyssa had been a quick study and had soon learned to separate vampire fact from fiction as she went about her life. The truth was that she could sleep anywhere and not have to rely on laying in the dirt of her birth, which she ruefully remembered, was not easy on her back. She did have fangs, but the only time they came out was to satisfy her bloodlust. You could see her reflection in any mirror, and the cross she proudly wore when out in public put a lie to that fable. She laughed to herself at the old saw about vampires turning into bats. Admittedly, the undead did have their ways when it came to transportation, and not being physically among the living did allow one to play fast and loose with space/time continuum.

To her often cynical/realistic world view, vampirism just sort of fit. She had few if any meltdowns in the beginning, nothing a pint of Type O Negative couldn't cure, and after about a ten-year shack down cruise, had a level-headed approach to being dead yet alive.

Alyssa's eyes glazed over. Her hand went to a place it often went in her private moments. She may be dead, but she was not dead. Outside of having a jones for bloodsucking, her mind and desires had survived unfettered by death. Alyssa was a vampire with fantasies and urges that needed to be dealt with. For Alyssa, sex had been a rollercoaster ride with her bloodlust always her copilot when she would go looking for someone.

Her memories were dark, erotically charged, and more than a bit funny.

There had been that night she encountered a guy who was a complete jerkwad, but as it turned out, was hung like a horse. He got his in about 30 seconds, leaving Alyssa to sulk. Alyssa got back at him by draining his body of every ounce of blood while he was in post-coital bliss and leaving him a bloody mess for the authorities to find.

Sometimes, things would get grotesque. Like when the blood urge hit her right in the middle of an acrobatic session with some Goth guy. She had found guys who played at being dark and scary to be the easiest lay. With his dying breath, he thanked her for teaching him what real horror was all about. Alyssa's assessment of that night had been that Mr. Goth had been good but not great.

Alyssa sighed. And then there had been the librarian she had met in a late-night coffeehouse. He was intelligent, good-looking in a Harry Potter sort of way, and was subtle and very smart in his seduction. They made love that first night, and then Alyssa did something she never did. She held back her bloodlust to the point of its own kind of ecstasy, kissed him on the cheek, and left. They would meet three more times. Alyssa was doing her best to hold back on her bloody urges, to the point where the word *love* was creeping into her mental vocabulary. On that final night, the sex would be blinding and extraordinary. Alyssa was over the moon, and in that blinding moment of heat, the vampire side broke through. She ripped into his neck, his screams of agony and orgasmic ecstasy blending into a final shattering scream as the librarian breathed his last.

Alyssa was both satiated and devastated. She covered his body with a blanket, kissed his forehead lovingly, and left the room, a tear-stained, emotional mess.

The tears once manifested themselves at the memory. Alyssa sank into the couch, sobbing. After a moment, she regained her composure. It was at moments like these that Alyssa thought about ending it all. Going out at the first rays of morning light and letting whatever sunlight would do to her just happen and end it all.

She had felt that way on occasion, during those dark moments when she realized that this was as good as it was going to get for all eternity. Could vampire suicide truly be the answer? Alyssa thought about spending this last night in contemplation and stepping out into first light. As always, she decided that she was not that brave and that this kind of life had to be better than what lay beyond.

Alyssa set the coffee maker for a fresh cup of black coffee to be ready and waiting when she awoke tomorrow night. Looking back into the darkness of the room, a smile showing teeth flashed for a moment. Then Alyssa turned…

…And was off into the night.

The End

Midnight Sabbath by Richard H. Fay

Spectral black hounds bay mournfully at the rising moon
To herald the arrival of the witching hour.
Vile creatures emerge from the deepening shadows
To pay bloody homage to their fell and fickle lord.

Sinister murmurs break the dreadful midnight silence
As tenebrous wraiths glide through a dismal yew forest.
Will-o-wisps flicker amongst the darkened branches
As a perverse and frightful procession passes below.

Imps dance a hideous jig beneath the mossy boughs
While goblin pipers play an evil discordant tune.
Wicked wights cavort wildly about a horned idol
While cowled figures gather 'round the gore-stained altar.

Malevolent voices chant a sacrilegious prayer
In anticipation of the nightly offering.
A winged abomination raises his keen-edged dagger
In a murderous act of diabolic sacrifice.

Devils and fiends revel in wretched debauchery
Until predawn's pallid light brightens the eastern sky.
Terrible rituals continue through the dim night
Until sunrise signals an end to the foul rites.

A Farewell by Marge Simon

She's dying.

Wise beyond her years,
bleeding tears, a drop of blood
from lips bound by secrets.

We bring tokens to grace
the chain around her neck.
I present a maple leaf,
Holbart, an onyx raven,
from dark Ammania,
a poppy fresh as dawn.

Her lover wears a suit worn thin
by years of use, unacceptable to us,
dusty as forgotten sins, but
she smiles and bids him near.

A ladies' man, a buccaneer --
we say his name, shake our heads.
He doesn't fit the scheme.
No vampyre -- is he something less,
or perhaps, something more?

He places his gifts upon her throat,
a tiny pirate's flag, a lustrous
histories unspoken,

black as his eyes.

Young Girls Are Coming to Ajo
by
Ken Goldman

The neon blinked erratically like a badly twitching eye: **VACANCY ... VACANCY ... VACANCYVACANCY ...**

Seen from the highway, the roadside motel off I-85 in Pima County did not fool anyone. It wasn't trying to. The old Papago Indian who ran the place hadn't bothered replacing the burned-out neon of the Canyon Motel's sign, and late-night motorists new to this godforsaken section of Arizona highway made no sense of the hot pink lettering that read "Ca yo Mo el." But that confusion dissolved with one look at the cabins. Visited more frequently by tumbleweeds than flesh and blood customers, here romance and candlelit dinners took a back seat to the sweat and stink of the genuine article. If you wanted pretension, for a few greenbacks more, there was the Carousel twenty miles up the road; if you preferred the down and dirty basics, you wanted the Canyon.

The muffler of Howard Corbin's rental had started bitching on SR143 South thirty miles out of Phoenix's Sky Harbor airport, nothing serious enough to warrant stopping for but sufficiently aggravating to frazzle the salesman's nerves by the time he entered the mining town of Ajo 130 miles outside Tucson. A tavern he approached called itself The Fork in the Road. Its front window logo shamelessly displayed a fork - the dining utensil variety - lying on the dividing line of a highway. What the place lacked in charm it made up for in ugliness, but in a town inhabited mostly by lizards, a beer is still a beer.

A few cold ones helped replace some of the hot piss inside Corbin with the more conventional kind; however, to really do the trick, there was only one thing. First, he called home to check on Edie and the kids before heading towards the bar to search for his curative.

The bleach job perched on the last stool clearly was a working girl, judging from the black hint of skirt she wore, an obviously uncomfortable second skin meant to look like silk but clearly wasn't. Too dark-toned to be a real blonde, she probably had a good ten years on him too, but when she caught his stare, he motioned to the bartender to freshen whatever the lady was drinking and ordered another cold draft for himself, reducing his introduction to the fundamentals.

"Hello. I'm Howard."

The woman clutched her long-strapped handbag as if expecting the man to lunge for it, but Corbin flashed his choicest balls-out smile at her. Normally, he would have added his surname, incorporating into his howdy-do the obligatory "... of Reinhardt & Reed Realtors, serving regions of the American Southwest." But that was not the business transaction Howard had in mind.

The woman thanked him for her white wine spritzer, barely looking up from her glass. She appeared reasonably sober, and that was good if she were game for a toss. At least she wouldn't be passing out later. When she spoke again, she almost managed to smile.

"Lilly. Let me guess. Salesman from out of town, right?"

"Seattle," he said.

"Like that dead racehorse?"

Bar talk. Wise-assed and meaningless. It always went the same.

"Well, welcome to Ajo, Mr. Howard-from-Seattle. It's where summer meets the winter." She smiled coyly.

"And what does that mean?"

"I haven't a clue. But it's on all the signs here."

"And Ajo ... does that mean anything?"

She grinned, seeming proud of her reservoir of knowledge. "Ajo comes from the Indian word *au-auho* ... it means red paint. The Sonoran Desert is covered in red sand, and the Papago tribe were great believers in cosmetics, wore lots of paint or something like that. Their Indian reservation still has a few residents just down the road."

"Tell them we're not giving them back Manhattan."

Her grin spread. "Those were the Canarsie Indians."

He had coaxed a smile from her, which meant he was home free even if this wasn't sparkling repartee. Once you passed your twenties, conversation from a barstool rarely entered that territory; into your thirties, you just tried not to sound pathetic.

He could tell the woman had been pretty once; maybe she had even bordered on beautiful. But the downslide had begun, and the gild was off this Lilly. Still, it was a seller's market tonight, and he was buying. They were two strangers sharing a patch quilt of irrelevant loungespeak that always precedes an excursion to a woman's underwear. Corbin had learned from years on the road to treat any barfly like a lady during the preludes. A woman seated alone on a tavern stool often had some pieces missing, so you had to prepare for anything if you were going to get into her pants.

When the conversation turned thin, Howard mentioned hosting Mr. Jack Daniels inside the trunk of his car, and the woman did not play dumb about his intentions. Moments later, Lilly sat cross-legged next to him inside the Escort, directing him to the first motel she saw alongside the dusty Sonoran Desert Highway. She murmured only "Here," and Howard dutifully pulled in.

Ca yo Mo el

[Blink . . .]

Ca yo Mo el

[Blink . . .]

Corbin hoped a nest of roaches would not come crawling from the bed linen, or worse, from his companion. Three other cars, each old and dirty, had parked outside the cabins, and that did not constitute much of an endorsement. Inside the small office, the dried-out Indian on the swivel behind the desk sat close to a small revolving fan that sent his long wisps of hair dancing. Mopping sweat from his silver-crowned pate, he never got out of his chair.

"One night?" the old guy asked, pivoting toward the Escort parked in the lot outside. He must have noticed the woman sitting in the front seat, but he gave no indication except to give his balls a healthy scratch.

Corbin nodded, deciding as he signed the register that his last name was now Smyth. He could have just as easily told him he would be staying for however long a good fucking took, for all the old fart cared. He looked at the Indian's name tag.

"Tuakam, is it?" he asked. "Did I say that right?"

"Tuck, they call me here. There's two of you?"

That covered the small talk.

"Yes."

"Number three's vacant, third cabin on the left. Close to the ice machine if you need it. Cash or credit?"

"Cash. Thanks."

Old Chief Plays-With-His-Nuts did not give a steaming turd about the nocturnal activities of the clientele he registered, and procuring forty dollars upfront concluded his portion of their transaction. The Indian reached up to yank a key from among several rows of them, returning his attention to the small black and white television that featured a pasty Mary Tyler Moore in an episode filmed years before lovely Mary had hit the wall.

Howard returned to the Escort. "The Indian who runs this place looks like he could use a good delousing."

"The Tohono O'odham Nation has a reservation nearby at Gila Bend. They're what's left of the Papago. They take the shit jobs around here because they work cheap. Indians manage a lot of the motels along here."

Howard nodded as if he cared and drove the Escort to number three, popping the car's trunk for his night bag and heading for the ice machine. At the cabin's door, he jumbled the key before the lock finally gave. Some former guest had given the ratty carpet a good soaking in piss, and the acrid odor assaulted him the moment they entered, but Howard doubted the other cabins smelled any better. He flipped the light switch and nothing happened. Corbin found his way to the nightstand and tried the lamp there. It worked although the bulb's wattage was low, bathing one wall a sickly yellow while leaving the rest in shadows. He turned on the air conditioner, a cheap and rusted window unit that banged and rattled.

The brass bed had surrendered to caked rust, and the spread, probably once green, covered a mattress that could have been solid granite. But the bed was a double, and Howard didn't care about anything else. He lay on it, scooting over to accommodate the woman. His shit-eating grin reappeared. Patting a pillow gone flat, he suggested she join him.

Lilly half-smiled, deep crow's feet spidering in the drab light.

"Business first, lover, okay?"

The statement, meant to sound easygoing, didn't. Smash-and-grab sex did not mix well with small talk. After all, this was business, and fucking strange men beat waitressing tables at Denny's, but it was still business. She was probably the wife of some blue-collar jerk, out to make some pocket change for herself. Howard fished five twenties from his wallet, and Lilly took his money. Examining the bills, she frowned.

Howard did not need a snake to bite him. "There's more if you're good, okay?"

"Oh, I'm good. Don't you worry about that." She stuffed the cash into her handbag and climbed on the bed, placing the bag carefully on the nightstand. "Would you like to undress me or should I do it myself?"

"Yourself. But slowly so I can watch."

She slipped off her black skirt, even threw in a little faltering squirm intended as some kind of erotic dance for Corbin's benefit. The attempt seemed pitiful, but even in these dry gulch towns, a hundred buys just so much. Kicking panties to the floor, the woman sat before Corbin naked.

Nearing the embarrassing perimeters of her forties, Lilly wasn't hard on the eyes, even in the unflattering light. Although her tits had begun to head south, they had some bounce. Her body seemed reasonably firm, too, but plum-colored varicose veins were already splintering from her ankles. She was almost completely shaven, except a thin landing strip, the type usually reserved for centerfolds and body-pierced Vampirellas, enough pubis remaining to suggest she had never been a natural blonde. She couldn't strip dance worth a shit either. Still, she wasn't a wasted hooker giving it away for a few drinks and cab fare. Some mileage remained on this woman's odometer, but not a whole lot.

"Think I can make it in Hollywood?" she asked, and it took a moment for Howard to realize that she was serious.

"Why not?" he lied.

Lilly's hand slid up his thigh, her touch coarser than he would have preferred. Still, Howard responded with a low moan, his hard-on reacting to the sensation of female flesh. Her tongue, considerably softer, followed the same path. When she took him inside her mouth, he felt he was going to release all of it right there. But she stopped cold, her grin reassuring him she wasn't about to bring it home just yet.

"So, Howard-from-Seattle, how would you like it? Squeaky clean, or just a little rough? I'm thinking maybe the latter?"

"Surprise me."

She reached into her handbag and pulled out two pairs of police-issue handcuffs, each polished to a high gloss. The manacles were the real item, not some tin trinkets purchased at some tacky sex shop. A roll of masking tape spilled out, too, but Lilly shoved it back into her bag, careful not to upset whatever else remained inside.

"Okay to use some of my toys?"

Howard's heart was racing now. He rarely had an erection throb so effortlessly since Edie was in her twenties, but a guy had to be careful in these situations. He quickly did the math. Hell, what was the worst that could happen? If the woman had anything unsavory in mind, it hardly mattered. He carried little cash, and the shitty rental parked outside wasn't worth stealing. If she wanted to roll him, she must have known there were faster ways to get money from him than sucking his cock.

"Let's play," he said.

Nodding approval, she cuffed him to the brass posts before he might have second thoughts. Howard's erection again sprang to life. Filling her mouth with ice, she went down on him but stopped just short of the decisive moment. Heaping more cubes into her hand, she slid them across his nipples, and in a gesture both odd and arousing, she took the same ice into her mouth.

She climbed on top of him, rubbing herself gently between his legs without taking him inside her. Rocking rhythmically, she coaxed his tongue into her mouth and teased him into a hot-blooded rush. She stayed with him, rising and falling in increasing undulations, and he hardened with each motion against her muff's soft bristle. Just as he felt sure he would come, she whispered, "Not yet ..." and eased him inside.

He wanted to feel her breasts, to fill his mouth with them, but his hands remained shackled. The power belonged to her as she pounded against his thighs, and her ass thrashed like some carnal animal. With her mouth against his ear, she spoke through quick and hot breaths.

"Now ..."

His body jackhammering hers, he spilled into the woman like hot ash. She filled herself with him, hips thrusting even after he came.

"Yikes, woman! You'll give me a heart attack!"

Howard lay still, trying to catch his breath, but Lilly had already climbed off and slipped back into her panties, standing by the night table without looking at him. She seemed to forget he was in the room while rifling through her handbag. Corbin realized the woman had switched gears and that his segment of the party was over.

"What are you--?"

"It has to be quick. Very quick ..." she muttered, not really speaking to him. She removed a large plastic container with something dark inside, but Howard could not tell what the lumpy object was. Suddenly uncomfortable with the thought that he remained cuffed to the bed, he pulled at the restraints, realizing he had zero chance of extricating himself.

[Christ, is she toting a gun in that container?]

Maybe she wanted to spatter his brains all over the piss-stained carpet just for the hell of it. In these small dirtwater desert towns, lunatic shit happened all the time just to give the local crazies something to do.

"Look, if it's money you want--"

The thing inside the container moved.

No gun ...

"I don't want any more of your money, Howard."

Popping the lid, she withdrew something alive that in the pallid light looked like an anemic dragon, a smallish thing that fit into her hand. The beady-eyed lizard, an ugly brown-spotted reptile that resembled a rat covered in snakeskin, displayed a mouth full of tiny pointed teeth. Howard had no idea what the woman was doing carrying around the oily bastard, but a single realization struck home. He had just fucked himself into one very tall pile of deep shit.

"Listen, I don't know what you --!"

The lizard tried crawling from her hand, but the woman stroked it from head to tail, and that seemed to calm the creature somewhat.

"Shhh! You'll frighten it. It won't do any good if you startle him. I'll have to wait for this little guy to calm down a bit, to get used to you."

"If you think I'm just going to lie here and wait for you to do God knows fucking what kind of kinky--"

The woman did not appear to hear him. She pulled out the roll of masking tape from her bag, tearing off a thick strip and covering his mouth.

"I'm sorry, Howard, I really am. I have nothing against you personally, but you came to me in the bar, didn't you?" She held the lizard close to his neck. "It's called a blue-tongued skink. Most come from Mexico and not many live in Arizona. An amazing creature, really. Pull off his tail, he grows another. The Tohono O'odham say they're easier to find right after they shed skin because they're more brightly spotted then. Have a look?"

"Mmmmmmphhh!!!"

Howard struggled against the bedpost, twisting and yanking the manacles until they scraped shrieking along the brass, his efforts to free himself making a lot of noise but serving no purpose.

"I know you're confused, Howard, but the skink is effective only after a woman has been laid because all that adrenaline is pumping and her vag is spilling over with seed. It's some sort of chemical thing, I think. The lizard doesn't do much for men, I'm afraid, but for women, the Indians say the skink offers a small piece of eternity."

She held the skink to her bare breast, allowing it to bite the soft flesh above her nipple, then pulling the unwilling creature from her and smiling, even as the tracks of fresh punctures leaked blood.

Barflies. They were batshit crazy and this bitch was their queen. Howard squirmed from the small snapping mouth, but the cuffs restrained any real movement. He could pull only a few inches from its fangs so the fucker would not sink its pinheaded incisors into his neck. She held the skink

46

closer to him, and something thick and crimson squirted from a sinus in its eye. It landed in a glob on Howard's chin.

Blood. It had to be.

"*Mmmmmmmmmphhh!!!*"

"Oh, he's angry, all right. He was aiming for your mouth, you know. They do that when they sense danger, a bad sign, sadly, according to Papago lore. They call it *Aak* when an animal becomes fearful in the presence of Man, but the skink is essential to their ceremony." She held the reptile against his throat. "This will be quick. I promise."

It was. The lizard snapped once, then sank its teeth into Corbin's flesh. Discovering the softest section of his throat, it redoubled its grip. With the hot seer of liquid venom, Howard gurgled, kicking and convulsing against the burning rush.

[No ... that's not quite right. Something else is happening here, something much worse.]

He heard the lizard gulp. The hot liquid was not rushing in. It was rushing *out*. The skink was sucking his flesh dry, drinking him! Engorged like a huge tick, the reptile was growing too fat and lethargic with blood to let go of its grip. Clutched against a thick vein in his neck, it continued to drink like an insatiable nursling.

Lilly's image fuzzed, but Howard had to watch her. The woman's voice seemed distant, her words dropping out as she spoke.

"Look at me, Howard. I know I'm not hard to look at, but would you call me beautiful? Not merely fuckable, Howard, but truly beautiful?"

Look ... Howard ... beautiful ...

Through the thick masking tape, Corbin struggled for breath, but the woman paid no attention. Every muscle was drying up inside him, every bone going to dust while the reptile held fast to his neck, a rapacious leech sapping its host.

The woman tried peeling the skink from his flesh, but the reptile clung stubbornly, and she had to pry its mouth open until the lizard released its grip. Fragments of shredded skin hung from its mouth.

"The Papago have this interesting philosophy about sharing, Howard. And for hundreds of years, their women have followed this ancient ceremony unknown to the outside world. We two have shared our bodies. My flesh and blood - and now yours - coalesce inside this simple creature ..."

She held the lizard close as if admiring the phenomenon of its existence. For a moment, it appeared the woman was embracing a cherished pet. Then she bit off its head, spitting the chunky remnant on the floor and drinking the dark blood spilling from the creature's neck. Squeezing out the thick soup of its innards, she swallowed the goo until the bloated reptile withered like an emptied sack. When she had finished, she wiped her lips with the back of her hand and inspected the *guano* dripping from her fingers.

The skink's shriveled torso lay limp and useless in her hands. She tossed it aside, smearing a dollop of the reptile's blood across each cheek, creating a freakish cosmetic hybrid neither rouge nor war paint. Touching Howard, she did the same to him, stepping back to regard her work.

"*Au-auho . . .*"

Her hands covered her face, the sharp nails shearing her own withered flesh in an act of self-mutilation. She peeled thick folds like dried cheese from her forehead and cheeks, a shedding snake throwing off her skin while revealing lumpy mounds of sopping membranous tissue underneath. The woman's features mutated into one breathing festering wound.

"*Au-auho* ... The red paint. First me, then you. We share all of it, you and I. The Papago believed all living things are related, there is an ebb and flow, a give and take, and all life is one. I doubt you understand, Howard, but that doesn't really matter now, does it?"

Lilly was correct. Corbin understood nothing, even while his body was folding in on itself, imploding like a child's deflated water toy. His vision on his right side went dark while something like a runny egg slid down his cheek, and Howard realized it was his eye. His remaining orb remained intact long enough to watch his flesh become a gelatinous, formless heap, the sizzling residual of warm gray mash smearing the faded sheets and trickling to the floor.

The dripping manacles hung from the bedposts, attached to nothing.

****

The old Indian's frown-wrinkled flesh did not easily accommodate his smile. But from behind the desk, he could not restrain himself as he studied the ravishing raven-haired, young woman who had entered the small motel office carrying a long-strapped handbag with thick blonde tufts of a wig that peeked through its snap. He nodded his approval. The first hint of crimson sun was rising in the Sonoran Desert sky, and even through the dust-caked windows, its rose glow caused the flesh of the woman to radiate like burnt gold.

"Thank you, Tuck," she said to him. "I know this was difficult for you to do for me again."

As can appear only on an aged face, there was sadness in the old man's smile.

"Lovely, the fluid smoothness of your skin, the sheen of your hair like black marble. Perfect in every respect. Winter again comes to summer in Ajo. The skink, he does good work," the Indian said.

"The lizard is rare and must be very difficult to find in these parts."

"Things hidden in the desert always are difficult to find. One must first know where to look."

The woman thought of the salesman from Seattle. Nothing much remained of him to find, that was damned certain.

"Yes. Well, thank you again, Tuck."

"Tuakam," he corrected her, as a doting parent might rebuke a discourteous child. "The young must always pay the aged the respect of a proper appellation despite the uncommonness of our circumstances, yours and mine. No man can alter this truth. You live not among our people, but the Tohono O'odham Nation forever remains inside you."

He was correct, of course. But the woman had always wanted more for herself than a life wasted on a primitive desert reservation. The elderly Indian never fully understood that, and seeing him again often muddied her own thinking with guilt.

"Forgive me the disrespectful habits of another world, Tuakam. The ancient ritual has a strange effect, and it becomes very difficult to know who I am … or even what I am."

The old man leaned forward to share a secret. "You are once more the beautiful woman you were. That is what you are. As to who you are, you need only to look into my eyes to know."

He took the handbag from her, placing the blonde wig and the stranger's belongings into a large plastic trash bag. Later he would burn everything, disposing of the man's car somewhere far in the desert. He looked at the register the man had signed the previous night. "Smyth. Probably not his real name," he said.

"No one will come looking. Not out here."

"Is the room cleared?"

"There's dust. A lot of it on the bed. It's all that remains of him, as with the others. And that smell. Always that damned smell."

"I will see to it," old Tuakam assured her. "Working here, I have learned another ancient cleansing ceremony that is even older than the ritual of the skink." He placed upon the desk a gallon container of Lysol. Together the Indian and the woman shared a remarkable moment of laughter.

There remained one final rite, and for this, the two turned serious. Each raised a palm to the other. Their open hands touched palm to palm, then slowly separated to conclude the ritual of parting.

"I must leave you now, Tuakam. Perhaps out there is a young brave like your father. I found him once. Perhaps this time, I may discover him again."

"Where will you go?" he asked.

"I don't know. Phoenix, for now, I guess. And should I grow restless, maybe after a while, when I can pluck up enough courage, I'll catch a bus to California and take that walk I promised myself. They call Hollywood Boulevard the street of dreams, you know."

Attempting to recapture his smile, the Indian reached below the counter and handed her a plastic container. Its lid had been punctured to produce several air holes. The dark lump inside shifted its weight. "For you, my mother. A small piece of eternity for when the time comes once more, as it must."

She placed the container into her handbag and kissed the old man's forehead, again parting from the son she had birthed nearly eighty years past.

Lilly did not look back as she shut the door behind her.

The End

The Dark Host by Richard H. Fay

Creatures of darkness roam this troubled night,
Drifting on the wind like an ebon mist.
Strange beings of shadow who shun the light
Gather in the hills for their savage tryst.

Whirring wings beat in the deepening gloom
As wicked sprites cavort atop the tor.
Wayward mortals face a terrible doom,
Joining the heinous host that they abhor.

Stolen children and lost souls swell the ranks
Of that wretchedly detestable horde.
A tithe of human flesh gives bloody thanks
To their dark and diabolical lord.

The unsanctified dead spread suffering
Until dawn's first glimmer drives them away.
No earthly force can stop their wandering;
The host is vanquished by the break of day.

Night Gallery

Rope on Fire

Review by the late Tom Johnson

- Rope on Fire
- Author: Mark Parragh
- Genre: Men's Action Novel
- Publisher: Waterhaven Media LLC
- ISBN: 978-1733975605
- Price: $14.95 (Paperback); $4.99 (Kindle); 324 pages
- Available at: Amazon and Google Books
- Rating: 5 Stars

"Smooth Reading, Plenty of Action"

John Crane worked for a secret government agency, the Hurricane Group, where he was a field agent until lack of funds shut down the group and left him out of a job. Then young billionaire Joshua Sulenski offers him a job. One of his projects he is funding is being harassed in Puerto Rico, and Josh wants him to find out who and why, and put a stop to the destruction of valuable equipment.

The first half of the book takes place in Puerto Rico where scientists are discovering microorganisms in the mud on the riverbanks. When men attack the lab wearing all black, Crane kills one of them and discovers they are cops. But they appear to be working for a Russian. He eventually stops the rogue police officers and Russian, but learns that someone else was heading the attack from the Czech Republic. The second half of the book takes place there, as Crane discovers a Russian crime boss behind the scenes.

This was a smooth read, with plenty of action. Well written and fun. Thankfully, there are no sex scenes to slow the story, and the use of profanity does not clutter the narrative, though there is some language. This was all about plot and characterization. Highly recommended.

Tom Johnson, author of *The Man in the Black Fedora*

Sarah and Zoey

Review by the late Tom Johnson

- Title: Sarah and Zoey
- Author: Linda Watkins
- Genre: Literary Fiction
- Publisher: Argon Press
- ISBN: 978-1944815066
- Price: $7.97 (Paperback); $2.99 (Kindle)
- Available at: Amazon and Google Books

> Rating: 5 Stars

"For Dog Lovers of Any Age"

Two women thousands of miles apart are brought into the life of a rescue dog named Zoey. Sarah Palmer, a writer for *The Globe,* loses her husband and son in a storm on a boat, leaving her broken and not wanting to live. Mindy Sue Watson is married to an alcoholic and wife beater. Unable to leave him, it ends in a final beating that almost takes her life until her dog, Zoey, comes to her rescue. She flees the house, but her husband catches the dog and drags it behind his pickup, almost killing it. Mindy reaches the hospital, and a neighbor calls the police about the man dragging the dog. Mindy's husband is arrested while she goes through several years of recovery. Zoey is turned over to the Humane Society and ends up where Sarah learns of the animal's history. She adopts Zoey, and during the next two years, she gets her life back with the dog's help. The writer in her wants to learn more about the dog's history and discovers the story of Mindy Sue. She takes Zoey on a road trip to visit his first "momma," only to discover Mindy living in a protective home, and her husband released from prison early. Bringing Zoey back to Mindy Sue puts them all in danger once more.

This was a wonderful story about a dog that helps two women in danger. It saves the life of one, and helps the other want to live again after great loss. For animal lovers, especially dog lovers, this story will tug at your heart. It's a short novella, and fast read, but the story moves smoothly and keeps the reader interested to the last page. Highly recommended.

Tom Johnson, author of *Wire Dog Stories*

Death Rides the Valkyrie

Review by the Late Tom Johnson

> Title: Death Rides the Valkyrie
> Author: Andrew Salmon
> Genre: Pulp Adventure
> Publisher: Timepiece Press
> ASIN: B012AA52O6
> Price: $.99 (Kindle); 68 Pages
> Available at: Amazon
> Rating: 4 Stars

The Valkyrie, Germany's greatest zeppelin, is flying over America showing their superiority over our air space. In New York, it takes on Tony Quinn and his aides, as well as Captain McGrath, who is publicizing the rehabilitation of a career criminal. This is to give plausibility to the plot. The trip plans stops in Chicago and Los Angeles. While en route to Chicago, a valuable ruby is stolen from a countess, and prints on the safe are revealed as those of the career criminal. But other things are happening. There appears to be a mysterious German team aboard, and one of them has a cloak of invisibility.

The whole story takes place on the airship, which gives it a fun read. The theft of the ruby is a red herring, however, and the real plot is the destruction of the zeppelin, with thousands of deaths, and clues to America causing the disaster.

The author switches roles with the aides a bit. Butch doesn't get to bang any heads together, and it's Silk who does the fisticuffs, while lovely Carol does the shooting (yeah, inside a gas bag). Plus, I didn't think the setting was a good choice for *The Black Bat*, though the story was well written and plotted. The magic cloak was a bit odd for the pulp character, too, though Germany was sure into the occult at the time; though the pulps usually tried to give explanations to the reader for mysteries like invisibility. And we're told that when the career criminal was rehabilitated, he was given new fingerprints. Really? That one I really wanted explained. But in the end, this was a fun read, and the author kept me involved in the story. Highly recommended.

Tom Johnson, author of *The Black Bat's War*

Mission: Prague

Review by the late Tom Johnson

- ➤ Title: Mission: Prague (International Espionage Thriller)
- ➤ Author: Nik Morton
- ➤ Genre: International Espionage Thriller
- ➤ Publisher: Manatee Books
- ➤ ISBN: 978-1544199902
- ➤ Price: 10.35 (Paperback); 292 Pages
- ➤ Available at: Amazon and Barnes & Noble
- ➤ Rating: 5 Stars

Tana Standish, now 38, was an orphan Jewish girl trying to escape Warsaw by sneaking on a ship with her brother. Her brother is killed trying to find food on the ship. She was also caught later, but before she is killed, a British submarine torpedoes the ship. The survivors include the young girl. MI6 learns that she has psychic abilities, and when she grows up, they train her as an espionage agent. She doesn't really read minds, but receives impressions, and can detect danger, hostile and friendly elements, as well as pick up hidden names. She is also studying remote viewing in connection to her abilities.

Mission: Prague is not her first assignment, but it is the first published tale about this psychic spy. It's 1975 and the height of the Cold War. Russia has their thumb on Czechoslovakia, and the underground has been broken. Britain sends Tana to Prague to help reestablish the underground, suspecting her own British organization may have a spy in their midst. Discovering something secret is going on at a mining camp, she plans to penetrate the mine and find out what's going on. But things go awry, and her every move has been watched. The underground is demolished, and she is captured and tortured. Now Russian intelligence may be able to open her mind for all the secrets she holds. The only chance she has is a rescue mission, but it's bound to be too late.

This is a new British espionage thriller set in the Cold War, and Tana Standish is a great new action heroine to be watched. The novel is topnotch, though the author goes off on tangents a bit too much in order to tie the story and people into real events. Still, if you are looking for a great new series, try this author out. You'll like Tana Standish, the psychic spy. Highly recommended.

Tom Johnson, author of *Assignment: Nina Fontayne*

The Choking Rain

Review by the late Tom Johnson

- Title: The Choking Rain "Book One of The Nemesis"
- Author: Brian Lowe
- Genre: Pulp Adventure/Mystery
- Independent Publishing Platform
- ASIN: B00T44SLHC
- Price: $2.99 (Kindle); 266 Pages
- Available at: Amazon and Google books
- Rating: 4 Stars

"A Fun Story"

Men connected to the Emerald American Railroad Company are dying in the rain from strangulation, as if an invisible killer is walking the streets of Los Angeles.

Detective-Sergeant Ted Kane is on the case. When millionaire Terence Aloysius O'Donnell's daughter, Mary, watches her fiancé die in front of her, Kane wants to question her. He's surprised to find her in the company of his best friend's sister, Katherine Reinhold, and with her in possible danger, he calls Eric "Captain Swashbuckle" Reinhold to come and help with the investigation. Eric brings along two more friends, T.J. "Professor Death" Gillis and Damien Pierrot. Together, the old pals tackle the mystery with Katherine's help.

The story is set during a heavy raining season in Southern California, as a mysterious brain behind a scheme kills to get what they want. The trail leads to the jungles of Brazil, giant snakes, headhunters, and a German camp of soldiers hidden from prying eyes. Can Captain Swashbuckle and his fighting team discover the secret mastermind and stop the strange deaths in Los Angeles before the Olympic Games?

There is some similarity to *Doc Savage, Pat Savage, Monk, Ham*, and *Renny*, and the adventure was fun. The story has a strong plot. However, at times the dialogue reminded me of *The Bowery Boys* or *Bud Abbott and Lou Costello*, but that's not bad, as I loved those characters. The running about tended to sound like *The Keystone Cops*, however, and the story read a bit slow; yes, there were plenty of things happening, but it just seemed to drag on and on without getting anywhere fast. And pulp stories should never drag. Still, this is a darn good plot, and I liked the characters, regardless of a few uses of wrong words and some problems with formatting – scene changes, mostly. Highly recommended.

Tom Johnson, author of *The Man in the Black Fedora*

Death Walks Behind You

Review by the late Tom Johnson

- Title: Death Walks Behind You
- Author: Andrew Salmon
- Genre: Pulp Mystery/Adventure
- Publisher: Timepiece Press
- ASIN: B0196AUPUO
- Price: (Free on Kindle); 76 pages

- Available on: Amazon
- Rating: 5 Stars

"For Pulp Fans and Lovers of Good Action"

Men of industry are being murdered, and then their factories are taken over by other firms. When Orson Woolcott III is killed nearby as Jim Anthony, Tom Gentry, and Jim's fiancé, Delores Colquitt, are returning to the hotel, Jim rushes to the murder scene and discovers a horrendous corpse bleeding out a form of mustard gas. It's the beginning of another great mystery to be solved, and a dire plot aimed at our fighting men in Europe.

I love stories set during WWII, and Jim Anthony was one of the better clones of *Doc Savage* back in the days of the pulp magazines. This story could have easily been published in the original pulps, as it read true to the original character. The story moves fast, and keeps the reader involved. I highly recommend this for pulp fans, and lovers of good action and adventure mysteries.

Tom Johnson, author of *Carnival of Death*

The Bread of Tears

Review by the late Tom Johnson

- Title: The Bread of Tears
- Author: Nik Morton
- Genre: Crime Thriller
- Publisher: Independent Publishing Platform
- ISBN: 978-1544123158
- Price: $12.75 (Paperback); 350 Pages
- Available at: Amazon and Barnes & Noble
- Rating: 5 Stars

Sister Rose returns to London after a speaking engagement, only to find murder at the hostel for the homeless. In an alleyway outside, she discovers the body of one of the girls she tended, brutally murdered, the sign of the cross carved in her chest. Rushing into the hostel, she finds two more bodies, also slain in a familiar manner. Sister Rose was not always a nun. She had once been a Newcastle police officer, but after a horrible incident that left her husband dead and her in mental straits, she had been secreted away to a hideaway run by nuns. There she had given her life over to God and made her vows. Five years later and these new deaths, and her mind wonders if they are connected to the old case.

There are several stories going on: the new murders in the hostel are connected to her past; the dead girl in the alley belongs to another murderer. There is the criminal empire involved in drugs and prostitution of young girls, and they will kill her if she intervenes. And to add to these problems, she may be having certain feelings for one of the investigators.

Wow, I found Maggie Weaver, aka Sister Rose, one tough nun. The author weaves the three stories together into a neat pattern, dropping Sister Rose into death traps that she must escape or suffer a horrible death, yet she holds to her faith as she struggles against great odds. In the end, she isn't afraid to send evil to Hell a little early. This was a fun read, and kept me turning the pages. The author's writing is smooth and the story flows easily. Highly recommended.

Tom Johnson, author of *Carnival of Death*

Lianne (Part II)
by
Linda Barrett

Ten:

Lianne had a great idea. I had to go along with her.

We stood overlooking the Raden. The sun started setting, casting golden sunlight over the fields atop the hill that we stood upon. That creepy turtle-shaped building loomed below in the valley among those apple trees. I tried not to sneeze at the incense burning from the hole on its ceiling. Lianne lowered her cloak's hood over her head. She glared at me with her emerald green daggers for eyes.

"Just watch me and do the same thing," she said in steely tones.

I had my eyes on the two bodies lying in the bushes.

"You didn't have to kill them!" I hissed.

"Well," she said, wiping the blood off of her sword's blade onto the grass, "What should we have done?"

"We could've tied them up and knocked them out!"

"They would have found them and gone after us!" She threw my hood over my head and handed me a gun. Its weight made my hand drop to the ground.

"Where'd you get this?" I asked, my voice quavering. "You can't buy guns in the People's Republic of the United States."

"It doesn't matter," she said through clenched teeth. "I have the sword." She reached behind her for the long weapon in her back holster.

I shook the gun at her.

"Guns are dangerous! They make a big noise and kill people. Sabin can take care of himself. He's got magic powers. Why can't he turn Ian Hand and his other weirdo friends into butterflies? Then they can fly away, and you and he can go together to Frisco and....,"

She unbuckled the sword and fastened it to my back.

"I'll take the gun." She shoved me along with her sandaled foot. "Knowing you, you'll miss him."

"At least, I won't wind up in jail for firearms possession!" I muttered through my hood.

She shoved me along the road. "Follow them," she said to me in a rough voice.

I shrugged and went down to the Raden. We bumped into the other weirdos who stood by its door. I heard them moaning and groaning in their funny language. Whatever they were moaning gave me the chills. The Holy Spirit told me to pray like a fiend that this thing would be over without too much bloodshed. Burning incense filled my nostrils, and I put my finger across my nostrils so that I wouldn't sneeze and make them look at me. I kept my head lowered while going around the winding temple stairs. I wanted to make sure that my feet wouldn't slip on the marble. These Uudah people sure had funny buildings.

We went up the stairs to the temple itself. The robed worshippers circled the altar in its center. I couldn't hold back my coughing for too long. Lianne shoved me again with her foot. I wanted to turn around and paste her in the face, but that would cause them to look at me.

The Sabin Lianne lay there on his or her back, eyes closed as if he or she was sleeping. She or he didn't make a move. She or he had on the jeweled belt and the whole shebang, really playing the role well. One of the robed weirdos picked up the dagger lying on the altar and raised it over the Sabin Lianne's head.

"*Ahnel cobida!*" he hollered and plunged the dagger into Lianne's stomach.

Lianne sat up and opened her or his mouth wide.

Kerunch!

Ian Hand had his head bitten off! The dagger fell out of his hand. All hell broke loose, and the robed weirdos ran in all directions. They were so scared they bumped into each other. I didn't know what to do.

Lianne grabbed me by my left arm and pulled me close to her.

"Give me your sword!" she hissed.

Pulling off my robe, she threw it behind me and pulled the sword out of its back holster. With both hands, she swung it at the high priests who ran down the stairs or jumped out of the Raden's windows. I ran up to the altar to save Sabin. He spat out Ian Hand's head and melted into something else. It made my knees quiver. He changed back into his handsome sword and sorcery hero form and jumped off the altar. Ian Hand started turning into something, too. His head and body stretched back into each other like Silly Putty.

In the next instant, Ian Hand turned into a dragon, shooting up to about ten feet tall. Sabin looked up and turned into a giant snake. You may think I'm crazy, but honest to God, that's what they did.

Lianne grabbed me with her free hand and dragged me away from the sight of the two creatures fighting it out.

"Let's go!" she shouted and pushed me towards the stairs.

"What about him?" I asked her when I regained my voice.

"Let's go!" she shoved me along. She paused to fight off some of the robed weirdos who stayed around to stop her from leaving.

Eleven:

A ruckus broke out. The people of Uudah, California, ran for their lives. Lianne found a horse and pushed me onto it. I had to hold onto her the whole time. My mind tried to figure out what was going on. Black magic is dangerous if you don't have the Holy Spirit in you.

Lianne rode like the horse was on fire. I just held on for dear life, praying that I wouldn't fall off.

"Why are we running away?" I shouted.

"To find something!"

She stopped the horse when we escaped from the crowds and got off at a museum. I stared at the building and figured out what it was. I read the sign on the museum's lawn next to its parking lot:

THE MUSEUM OF THE CHRISTIAN FAITH.

Somehow, it dawned on me that she listened to my talk about Jesus and decided to believe me. She didn't say a word as she ran up the handicapped wheelchair slope and banged on the ornate golden doors. I just sat on the horse and watched her. She burst into the doors, and in a few seconds, she came out again with the biggest cross she could find in this weirdo, New Age state. It shone in the setting sun like a beacon. My heart soared with joy.

"What do you plan to do with that?" I asked, choking with tears.

"Never mind," she snapped and hoisted herself into the horse's saddle.

We rode back towards the Raden, passing deserted towns and roads. I held onto the crucifix, weeping the whole time.

God had not abandoned us. Even in this terrible time, He didn't let us down.

Stopping the horse, she snatched it out of my hands and ran towards the building.

By this time, Sabin morphed into a dinosaur, something called a Tyrannosaurus Rex, and Ian Hand morphed into a giant squid. They battled each other, changing into each fierce and weird animal, creatures you see in all these nature documentaries on educational television.

Lianne held up the cross, and I got down and knelt beside her. I shut my eyes at the horrific sight and prayed my heart out.

Sabin shrunk down, and Ian Hand turned back into a giant human. He opened his mouth, and Sabin jumped into it. Ian Hand made a grotesque face, and his eyes rolled. He wheezed and coughed up mucus. Ian Hand shrunk back down and zipped back into the Raden's skylight.

Lianne and I ran into the Raden, climbing up the stairs. She still held onto the crucifix. When we reached the temple's center, we found Sabin climbing out of what was left of Ian Hand. She threw down the cross and ran to him into a loving embrace.

"The god that you worship gave us the power to conquer Ian Hand. When I looked at your cross and the faith you have in your god, it gave me the idea. I would like to thank you," Lianne said to me.

"Aw, shucks." I laughed and blushed under my furry face. "It was nothing!"

The California State police burst in with their guns trained on us. They took us into custody, and I made a phone call to Sunshine to bail me out and send me home. I made the people of Uudah, California, better off without their kooky, spooky leaders. I don't know what happened to Lianne and Sabin, but they must have lived happily ever after like they do in all those romance novels.

The End

Old Man's Elixir by Matthew Wilson

Fear of death has made me drink the tea
Mixed with the blood of my ancestor great
Tepish who bled prisoners of his victory
Whose hunger grows within me without sate.

Haiku II by Denny E. Marshall

werewolf claws
escape alive
face on floor

The Black Eyes of Ulspruth-Dimot
by
Lee Clark Zumpe

A misty morning met the awakening village of Madichi. Dawn made pale the cloudy skies, and upon the breeze cascading down from the mountains was a subtle chill. The brooding men and pensive women of the village set about their chores, taking up their labors in the field, in the home, and in the market. As the sun rose, limping up into the sky and away from the purple mountains, the mist slipped out of sight, and night was at last completely behind them.

This was so, except about the peak of one solitary old crag. Coiled about the summit of this lumbering mass of jagged granite was a peculiar crown of mist, a wispy ring of clouds that seemed to encompass a small haven of darkness.

It was upon this mountain, within this darkness, that dwelled the thing they called Ulspruth-Dimot. No one knew what it was, nor from what infernal lair it had come, nor even how many eons it had nested there upon that peak, but almost everyone in the village of Madichi agreed that it was something to be feared.

Few of the villagers that day bothered to greet a company of Iymeridians who came marching through the center of town around mid-morning. Clad in fine armor, with leather breeches and mail shirts, they streamed in off the long road to Ghatlynn and made their way toward the market square. From their sides hung dirks and longswords, and upon their backs were round wooden shields. Some of the red-haired giants carried great battle-axes.

There was not a smiling face amongst them. Each and every one appeared grim and withdrawn, their moods somber and serious.

As the solemn procession glided past the villagers' homes, pastures, and gardens, there were some who frowned and some who muttered words beneath their breath and to the ground so that they could not be heard. There were some who shook their heads and some who simply turned away.

Rashybha and Tya beheld the legion as it trudged along.

"Another helping of silage for the Lord Atop the Mountain," said the silver-haired haggard old woman named Rashybha. She was busy tending to a patch of vegetables outside her tiny cottage when she heard the steady tramp of soldiers' boots on the gravel road. Having lived in Madichi for all her years, the old woman had seen the passage of a dozen such armies. "Just another feast for Ulspruth-Dimot."

Another woman, a young maiden named Tya, leaned against a split-rail fence. She admired the handsome lads of the Iymeridian troop as her red locks tossed in the breeze. Upon hearing Rashybha's comments, she grimaced at her elder.

"It's not right," she began, "To speak of them in such a way." She turned toward her neighbor, who was squatting in her modest garden and keeping herself busy. "At least these brave men have the courage to face the Crawling Worm atop that mountain. The men of Madichi shudder at the very mention of that thing, and they cower behind their doors at night and keep their gaze from the mountain as though the mere sight of it could in some way bring them doom! If only our village possessed the kind of courage that must flow through the blood of these heroes."

"What does courage matter if their crusade is predestined to failure?" Rashybha met Tya's gaze, and the lines in her forehead deepened. Her empty eyes and pale face spoke of the ageless terror that haunted her always. "Can mere courage succeed where a hundred swords and a thousand warriors pure-of-heart have failed?"

"The death of a courageous soul is far more honorable than the withering demise of a fearful one."

"Death comes to both the valiant and the fearful ... why should one hasten it?"

"They risk their lives for you, do you not see that?" The red-haired young woman finally shrugged and turned back toward the Iymeridians. "Without the bravery of soldiers such as these, how can the village hope to survive another winter under the watchful black eyes of Ulspruth-Dimot?"

"You put too much faith in your beaming young lads. Look into their eyes as they shamble by, and you will see neither pluck nor mettle; you will see fear, for they know well that death awaits them at the summit of that mountain." The old woman paused and pursed her lips. Tya was a stubborn child, and her resolve was not easily shaken. "You seem to be full of energy and courage," said Rashybha, "Why not join with your noble young soldiers and slay the Crawling Worm atop the accursed mountain?"

Tya had no response to offer Rashybha, but there was no doubt that she had heard the words.

****

The dawn of the following day sent night scattering once more into shadows and into the deep hollows between the towering mountains surrounding the tiny village of Madichi. The rays of the sun streamed down over the crest of the mountains, bathing the valley with light.

But atop the nearby mountain, upon a broad rock-strewn plateau, a patch of mist refused to dissipate and a pool of darkness scoffed at the rising sun. While in Madichi, the farmers tended to their crops and their livestock. In the market square, the shop-keeps took inventory of their stocks and prepared for a day of business; the writhing bodies of a legion of Iymeridians gasped and wept and prayed for the darkness to retreat.

Pitifully, the bloodied soldiers tried to drag themselves from the scene of carnage. There were a few dozen of them left, only a handful of the original contingent. Terror and fear mixed in their wide eyes. Masks of desperation clouded their faces.

Merciless flies swirled over a mound of carcasses as a river of steaming, frothy blood streamed from its base. Other corpses, mutilated and unidentifiable, were strewn across the plateau. Their chests had been torn open, their organs had spilled to the ground, and their bones had shattered and jutted forth from bluish flesh.

It was onto this scene that a young, red-haired maiden arrived.

Tya picked up a sword from a dead warrior, raised it high in the air, and cried out the name of the cruel god.

"Ulspruth-Dimot! Here is one more mortal body upon which you may feast!" The surviving Iymeridians cringed. They spoke out, trying to silence her, trying to warn her, but she did not hear them. "I offer up this flesh freely, for I know someday you will eat so many mortals your belly will burst open and you too will suffer!"

The Iymeridians, convinced that Tya was either a fool or a lunatic, began to distance themselves from her. She stood firmly, swinging the sword in the air above her head, drawing circles in the darkness.

Soon, the mist began to stir, and a cold wind thrashed over the plateau, carrying upon its breath a horrid stench. All the wounded Iymeridians could think to do at that moment was scream, and scream they did.

If the sun yet shown beyond the boundaries of that mountain top, not a soul upon it would have known.

The mists parted as Ulspruth-Dimot slithered through the shadows. Tya caught brief glimpses of its form as it circled her over and over. Its skin was bony-white, the white of the full moon on high. Its worm-like body appeared enormous and bloated.

Tya heard the death-calls of the Iymeridians whose anxious flight had placed them in the beast's path.

There was an instant of silence before Ulspruth-Dimot struck.

And then, the yawning black pit of its mouth swooped down through the mist and hovered inches above the tip of Tya's sword. A ring of jagged teeth encircled its orifice, and a foul darkness bubbled forth from its pithy throat and dribbled like slaver over its quivering lips.

All these things were terrible enough, but its eyes...

Its eyes were deeper and darker than any moonless night Tya could recall. They were the very essence of evil and hatred. They were the very color of dread. In those pools of black, death loomed.

It was the piercing horror of those eyes that had sapped young soldiers of their confidence and stripped proud knights of their valor, paralyzing them with fear and inducing fatal indolence and insignificance.

Yet, Tya did not falter nor tremble nor cry out. She stood before the awesome monster that had inspired such mind-numbing and life-draining fear amongst the villagers of Madichi, and she was not afraid.

In one sweeping motion, Ulspruth-Dimot swallowed the young maiden whole.

As she slid down the slimy length of its throat, Tya took the sword and thrust it deep into the inner lining of the beast. She felt the blade sink deeper and deeper, and she could feel the sudden response of the monster.

It reeled back, sending the mists about it swirling. It coughed, sputtering up blood and half-digested bits of Iymeridians ... vomiting bones and limbs and torsos. It thrashed to and fro, trying to dislodge the sword from within its throat, but its struggles proved futile. Eventually, it slumped forward and heaved up one last wail before dying.

Tya crawled from the great gaping maw of the monster and staggered back toward the village wordlessly. The mists that had skirted that mountain for eons were fading; and, the rock-strewn plateau that had known no hint of sun since the dawn of time now welcomed its light.

The Black Eyes of Ulspruth-Dimot closed forever.

The End

Alice, Vampyre by Marge Simon

Alice parts the curtains on the eve ahead,
wishing for a glimpse of cobalt from the sinking sun,
a sight she treasured on the shores of Piracus,
so many centuries ago, when she was young,
unaware that her mortality was soon to change.

City of Rats
by
Todd Hanks

While flying over a dump, the scientist in a white lab coat, leather hat, and bug-splattered goggles saw three rats, each as large as a small dog, gnawing on the remains of a blood-drenched human. His triangle-winged ultra-light aircraft had three wheels. High pitched engine whine, light smoke trail, the plane was as yellow as mustard and had a finback tail. Having left his underground laboratory, he soared like a turkey buzzard above a poisonous pasture and rusty river's bend. His fingers rested lightly on the joystick of the ultra-light, tilting the wing into the roaring wind. He skimmed the plane low, searching for live humans, then again rose, like a yellow petal blown in a gaseous breeze.

The scientist flew over trash canyons, vestiges of a civilization of long ago. *It's ironic that the pollution wasn't the downfall of humanity,* he thought. *As it turned out, we could live in our own garbage in our last city like cockroaches. The rats were the downfall, as with the black plague.*

But it hadn't been a plague. Some scientists long ago had altered rats' DNA, creating long-living creatures with ultra-intelligence and super strength. Scientists such as he had bred the rats for centuries, and they were the one reliable food source for humans. Although there were over a million of these rats, they all had the same mother, and all were male. Deterioration was stopped in the mother rat, and she had been made immortal. She had been alive for centuries but had changed. Her head had mutated over the years to that of a spider, with horned mandibles where her snout had once been, and she had six legs. The mother rat grew to the size of an obese human, with a hairless bulbous stomach and many large red eyes on her forehead. The spider-like rat constantly mated with its offspring.

An earthquake had freed the rats from the lab. They had carried off their mother to a hidden location and had begun attacking the populace. The entire city had already been dismantled by the quake, and the people were already panicked. Soon they faced a new horror, for these rats could chew apart a human in seconds.

****

Cliff Cyrus had barricaded himself inside a warehouse, hiding from human predators and squads of rats. The storehouse had been the find that saved his life. There were piles of canned foods and crates of bottled water. The only windows were up by the ceiling, where shafts of light exploded into the warehouse during the day. *Think about it,* Cliff considered. *Weeks ago, I was a food deliverer. My life was normal, even dull. Now I exist by crouching hidden in a warehouse, like a rodent myself, with a winter's supply of food in his burrow.*

He had existed for weeks in the small car he used for delivering food. When the rats had pulled people down in the streets, Cliff had found a hiding place for his car behind a billboard and a row of trashcans. He had curled up in his leather jacket and smoked, eating the food from his delivery oven. The food had run out before the cigarettes. He was finally forced to scout around, avoiding herds of rats. The streets and buildings appeared to be deserted, but twice he caught sight of children that quickly disappeared in the piles of refuge that had lined the streets for centuries. He found he was only blocks away from a small store, broke into the little building, and took food and smokes. He found a baseball bat behind the counter, picked it up, and carried it back to his car with the bags of looted goods.

One night, he was attacked, but not by rats. Three ragged men found his car and busted out the windows. Cliff emerged swinging the bat, catching one man in the side of his head. He busted another in the knee. But the third man pulled out a pistol and shot. Cliff felt the bullet scrape by his chest. The young man ran as fast as he could. A day later, he found the warehouse. The door was unlocked. Cliff entered, checked out the place, and found it was empty. He locked the door behind him and had not left since.

****

The scientist in the ultra-light aircraft had never flown this far from the city. He saw no trace of civilization. The pilot steered through radioactive snow. The flakes lightly burned the skin of his face, and soon he looked as if he had been too long in the sun. Next, he flew over the sand dunes of a desert, on which sometime in the past people had made small mountains of discarded clocks. *I need to go back to the city and search again,* he thought. *I don't think there are any people on the outskirts.* He landed to refuel from a container he carried. The desert's silence seemed to intensify under the mountains of motionless clocks as if time had stopped.

****

Every night Cliff could hear the armies of rats outside, scuttling by the thick metal door. He would lie on a blanket and ensure himself there was no way they could get in. Then one night, he heard a girl hollering, pounding on the door to the warehouse. "If anyone's in here, please let me in!" she screamed. "They're coming! The rats are coming! Please, someone help!"

Cliff leapt to his feet and pulled open the door. A young woman ran inside, wearing a short red dress that was half-torn off her shapely body. Her hair was bright pink in the moonlight that streamed through the door. Suddenly, Cliff was pushed backward as several rats shoved into the open entrance. The young man shut the door, grabbed the baseball bat, and slammed back one rat that had turned to attack. The rodents were the biggest he had seen yet. These rats were almost the size of armadillos, with fangs like cobras. The young woman screamed. Cliff grabbed her and pulled her back toward some shelves. Three rats followed, moving slowly, stalking the humans.

"You can't fight them all with that bat," said the woman in a shaky voice.

"I've got a backup plan," said Cliff.

He had, of course, searched the storehouse for potential weapons and had found the insect repellent in the back, heavy-duty canisters. Cliff picked up one can. He sprayed it toward the rats while flicking a lighter and holding it lit up to the long stream of fluid. The insect repellent canister was transformed into a flame thrower, shooting a long burst of fire across the room, catching the hair of all three rats and engulfing their twisting bodies into flame. All three writhed, screamed, and screeched until dead.

****

Once again above the ramshackle city, the scientist saw herds of rats crawling toward what was once the state Capitol. It *must be where they've taken the mother rat,* he thought. He landed on the long flat roof of the state Capitol building and pulled a pistol from under the seat of the aircraft. The scientist found a door to a stairwell and worked his way down through the building until he heard thousands of teeth gnashing. The hallway was empty. The scientist looked through the window to the door to where Congress had once held session. Rats filled the entire room, piled on top of each other on the plush red chairs. But the aisle was clear to the front, where the spidery mother rat sat behind a bench as if on a throne. Her many red eyes glowed, and her legs waved in front of the bare pink orb that was her stomach.

****

"What's your name?" asked Cliff, looking into the eyes of the beautiful girl.

"I'm Rachel," she said. "Thank you for saving my life."

"Don't mention it," he replied. "My name is Cliff. Where did you come from? You don't see too many people who are alive on the streets these days."

"A large number of people have gathered to live under the city," said Rachel. "I can take you there. I just got cut off from the manhole. I was foraging and got separated from my friends. A ladder in the manhole leads down to the camp below. I don't think the rats can climb it, and we have the other entrances to the tunnels sealed off. We are preparing to fight them. Now, I can tell them to make flame throwers. Will you come with me? My friends will be most grateful you have protected me."

"Sure," replied Cliff. "But why don't we wait till morning to leave?"

The girl smiled in agreement, and they cuddled together under the blanket for the rest of the night. In the morning, Rachel took him to the manhole. He climbed down and was led into an area where thousands of people had pitched tents. Small campfires burned in trashcans. Rachel told the people about her rescue, and Cliff was treated by everyone as an honored guest. When they heard of the idea concerning homemade flamethrowers, they sent out foragers to find flammable canisters. Soon, they had an army of men and women with flamethrowers and backpacks full of canisters. They walked down the city streets on one appointed night, making bursting red conflagrations out of rat battalions. The blood tide of the war had turned. Mankind was once again a hunter. Rachel and Cliff fell in love while in the chaos of battle, and within months became betrothed.

****

The scientist knew he would only have one chance. He stormed through the door of the room in the state Capitol building and rushed the aisle, holding the pistol in front of him. Rats screamed and squealed from red chairs. But the man got off a shot, dead center in the mother rat's forehead. He felt the teeth of her offspring tearing into his knees and shins. He shot again into the tight stomach of the mother rat, blowing a hole in her the size of a baseball, sending a firework-high fountain of black blood, and chunks of pink and gray flesh catapulting from her bulbous belly. The mother rat fell forward, quivered, then lay still. Her children leapt onto the scientist from all sides. "You'll die off now, too!" he shouted. His vision went black as they piled in heaps onto his falling form. "You can't reproduce now. You'll die off now, too!" He gave one more muffled, defiant scream, feeling fangs in his sides and neck and tasting rat hair.

The End

The Devil's Highwaymen by Todd Hanks

Where the highwaymen ride
the air is always chilled.
Darkness is placed like a lid
on the surrounding hills.
Blackbirds land on bones of trees.

They are the devil's highwaymen.
No one escapes their guns.
They have ridden this trail of blood
every night since hung.

For very successful ventures
of plundering gold,
while alive they sold their souls.
Now they ride the devil's road
every evening for eternity.
Nights of murder and thievery
add to Satan's treasury.

Long boots, coats with tails
and wide lapels, black masks
that cover just around red eyes.
Long powder pistols at their sides.
Capes and sabers. Transparent as vapors.

Their phantom horses prance
through swirling, winter mist, the
hazy lights of Dublin in the distance.

Closing the Deal
by
Lee Clark Zumpe

Stan cracked the front door and glared at the little man standing on his porch. He tipped his head to the right, and watched as the scrawny salesman read the NO SOLICITING sign through squinting eyes behind bottle-thick glasses. The evening thunderstorm had tapered off into a soft drizzle, but the salesman had clearly been caught in the summer downpour. The long sleeves of his button-down shirt stuck to his bony arms, and his shoes made squishing sounds as he shifted weight from one foot to the other.

"Beggin' your pardon, sir." Awkwardly, the salesman forced himself to make eye contact with Stan. Rivulets of water cascaded down from his matted hair over the acne-pocked landscape of his face. Even as he spoke, a bead of water rested on the rim of his upper lip, dangling and quivering with each breath. "I'm not here to sell you anything you don't want."

"That's what they all say," Stan grunted. Stan stood in the doorway like some ancient Roman statue guarding a shrine. Skirting the uppermost borders of middle age, his hair had thinned and grayed over the last decade, and his once youthful expression had begun to deflate. Still, he exercised daily; he kept lean and fit. He remained the envy amongst the remnants of his teenage clique, a constant reminder that they too could have kept themselves from swelling into soft, lumpy, bitter loafers. Stan eyed the salesman, his face curling itself into a disclosure of his disgust. "Take it next door, buddy – there's a woman there who'll drop a twenty for just about anything."

"You don't understand, sir," the salesman stammered, summoning up the most imposing voice he could. He leaned in toward the doorway, tried to position himself to keep Stan from slamming the door in his face before he could cast his bait. "Despite my appearance, I don't just go door to door. No, I'm better organized than that. In today's world, you have to be very familiar with your potential markets. You have to know your clients intimately. You have to react to their needs promptly."

"I don't follow…"

"Point is, sir: If I show up at your door, you must have summoned me." The salesman coiled his lips up into an unsettling grin. "If you'll permit me a few moments of your time, I'd be happy to explain."

Stan shook his head.

"I've got too much to do to waste the time … like I said, the woman next door,"

"I'm not interested in the woman next door." The salesman backed away from the door, swayed back in his shoes so that he could see the next house down the street. "She has nothing to offer me at this time, and I can offer her nothing. Therefore, we have no business to conduct. I understand she drove her husband off a few years ago – cheated on him with some drunk she picked up down at the Rusty Nail Tavern, didn't she?" He shrugged. "To each her own, I suppose."

"How'd you know…"

"She doesn't like you very much, I gather. You're the one that tipped her husband off, aren't you?"

Stan nodded, smirked mechanically. The thought of it filled him with a sick sense of satisfaction. He had hated having to break the news to the man who lived there, but …

"How do you know all this?"

"Like I said, you have to know your clients intimately …"

Ten minutes later, Stan and the salesman sat at his dining room table. The salesman had declined the offer of a cold soda, but he did accept a towel from the linen closet to mop up his soggy clothes.

Gluttony
Saturday, 1:10 a.m.

Midnight washed away half the patrons at Just One More, a seedy little bar on the outskirts of town near the rows of dilapidated warehouses and processing plants that had been abandoned when all the corporations moved to Mexico in search of cheap labor. Stan arrived as the lightweights were pulling out of the parking lot, swerving down the two-lane highway toward nearby trailer parks and cheap motels. His timing was intentional. Being nocturnal animals, crack pushers rarely closed deals in crowded pubs, no matter how sordid and sleazy their reputation.

Stan sat at the bar nursing a warm beer, perched on a barstool, trying not to touch anything. The place was crawling with cockroaches. The bartender intermittently smashed a line of ants besieging a bowl of peanuts on the bar. Afterwards, he would wipe their tiny corpses across his apron.

After only a few minutes, two scrawny men in white T-shirts disappeared into the bathroom. Stan stood, followed them.

Through a slit in the door, Stan watched as one coughed up a wad of bills. In exchange, the other handed him a plastic sandwich bag which he stashed in his jeans pocket.

Back out in the bar, Stan did not bother to put his glasses on as the men returned to their respective tables. Instead, he held them up to his face, peering through the lens cautiously. The tint of bluish skin shocked him, but it was the rolling of the flesh, seemingly displaced by a multitude of vermin just beneath the surface, that made him cringe and shudder.

"Hey," Stan said, slapping a ten-dollar bill on the counter. He glanced toward the jittery addict across the room. "You know that guy?"

"Think his name's Trevor," the barkeep said.

Back in the comfort and security of his car, Stan added Trevor's name to the list.

****

"Nice place," the salesman said absently. He looked around the room, at its Spartan décor, at the eggshell white walls that spread out in every direction. Stan's house had an overwhelming and overpowering element of neutrality about it. He had never been one for accoutrements and ornamentation. "Life has enough distractions of its own. No need to pin on any more to your environment, right, Stan?"

"I guess."

"Well, look around you. I can see by the way you keep your house so neat, so organized, that you do not believe in that modern notion of amassing material possessions." Stan eased himself into a self-assured smile, not having given much thought to it. He squirreled away as much money as he could from each paycheck, paying the mortgage, picking up enough supplies to last him until the next payday. He had plain furniture, white blinds, and dull drapery over his windows, drab gray carpet blanketing the floor of the house. "Keep it plain and simple, no attachments, right, Stan?"

"It doesn't seem necessary."

"Precisely – and that's a very ancient concept, one that not many people understand these days. Aside from food and shelter, everything you really need is housed inside your skin."

"I suppose so. I've always thought the best investment you can make is keeping yourself in good shape."

"That's true, Stan – that is absolutely true." The salesman leaned forward, resting both arms on the dining room table, slanting forward in his chair as if he was about to whisper something to Stan that he did not want anyone else to hear. "And the shape you're in – physically – is a reflection of the state you're in morally."

"Well, I don't…"

"No – think about it, Stan." The salesman bounded up from his chair and circled the table. "If a man can't be trusted to maintain his only important possession, how can he be expected to maintain his integrity, his decency? If a woman lets herself go – doesn't take care of herself, doesn't keep in good condition, how can she be expected to preserve her virtue?"

"What do they say, your body is your temple?"

"Exactly. You don't have to go far to see it. Look around you. Immoral behavior, perversities, wickedness, and corruption – they all show right through the skin, Stan. Sin is a form of decay, and though the decay may begin deep inside, at the core – eventually, it makes its way to the surface." The salesman stopped in front of the window, peeled back the curtain a few inches. "Look out there, look at your neighbors. You *can* judge a book by its cover. You know who the sinners are!"

Sloth
Friday, 5:30 p.m.

"It's not my responsibility, ma'am." The expressionless pharmacist stood on the opposite side of the counter, one hand pocketed and the other fidgeting with a pencil. "You'll have to call your doctor's office and have them prescribe something else. Your insurance doesn't cover this brand."

"I already spoke with the lady receptionist," the elderly woman said, leaning against the counter for support. A line had formed behind her. Stan stood at the back, waiting to pick up his monthly allotment of beta-blockers to control his high blood pressure. "She said that everything would be taken care of."

"Well," the pharmacist said, frowning, "she apparently doesn't understand the paperwork. Your husband's plan doesn't include brand name medication of this nature,"

"Of this price, you mean?" The old lady's unexpected barb visibly rattled the pharmacist. "If you would just call the doctor, I am sure that they could straighten all this out."

"It's not our policy, ma'am," he said, dismissing her. "I have other customers."

"What about this prescription? My husband needs it …"

"I've told you what to do ma'am."

"But it's after hours! I don't know if I'll be able to get anyone at the office …"

"Next, please."

Stan slipped the glasses the salesman had given him out of his pocket. Through their telling lenses, he saw the slate gray hue of the pharmacist's flesh, the featureless expression which lacked both eyes and ears. There he stood, a monument to indifference, a cold, marble sculpture devoid of compassion and empathy.

When Stan reached the counter, he read the pharmacist's nametag and made a mental note of it for future use.

****

"So," Stan said, "You're selling religion…"

"Oh, no, Stan: Religion isn't something you can acquire through some form of business transaction." The salesman shook his head, frowning at the very thought of it. "You either have religion, or you don't. You can't pick it off a clearance shelf at the outlet mall any more than I can peddle it door to door."

"What then? Exercise equipment? I'm sorry to disappoint you, but I don't need..."

"Wrong again, Stan; but I'll give you points for trying." The salesman sat down across from Stan, retrieving a notepad from his breast pocket. Simultaneously, he produced a small carrying case which he placed at the precise center of the table, opening it with a moderate tap and revealing a pair of tortoise-shell horn-rimmed glasses with unusually thick, smoky lenses. "I do hope you'll forgive the outdated style. What they lack in aesthetics they make up for in utility."

"Glasses? You want to sell me a pair of reading glasses?"

"Absolutely not," The salesman kept one finger hovering above the glasses, the digit swaying gracefully from side to side to affect an almost hypnotic phenomenon. He scribbled a few lines on his notepad, glancing at Stan occasionally, as if recording certain physical traits and general impressions he deemed worthy of cataloging. "No, sir. In fact, these are our gift to you." He paused, dropping his pen. "Doesn't seem like much of a gift at face value, does it Stan?"

"Not really."

"You'd be surprised at just how valuable those glasses can be. And by value, I mean fiscal value," the salesman said, a decidedly sly smile spreading over his face. "You see, my organization seeks out individuals with acute observational skills – expert insight and acuity regarding the human condition. We consider your gift of perception a valuable resource and we would like to take advantage of it. What's more," the salesman said, narrowing his eyes to accentuate his offer, "we intend to compensate you for your contributions."

"I already have a job," Stan said. "I enjoy what I do."

"That may well be, Stan." The salesman nestled his chin into the palm of his right hand. His index finger tapped the pallid flesh of his cheek as he considered his next line of reasoning. "It's really a pity, you know. A man like you, thrifty, prudent, spending years saving money. Yet, here you are. You've come to a realization in the last few months, haven't you, Stan? You can't afford this place anymore, can you?"

"I've never missed a mortgage payment," Stan said coldly, all trace of affability obliterated. The salesman reminded him of covetous bankers questioning his ability to match the annual rate increases. "I'll decide when it's time to put this place up for sale."

"I think you already have, Stan," the salesman said, allowing his gaze to wander around the room, mocking the interest of prospective buyers. "Maybe you haven't been completely truthful with yourself about the decision, but I think that you've already made it. Rising property taxes, increasing insurance rates – it's a disgrace that an honest, sensible, practical man like you can't even manage to preserve the American dream."

"Times are tough," Stan said, echoing the resilience of generations of Americans who faced similar hardships. "Things will get better."

Greed
Saturday, 8:17 a.m.

"I'm sorry, Stan." Lou Masters had worked with Stan for years, refinancing his mortgage and monitoring his IRAs. "Looks like this market has just priced you out. As your financial advisor, I think that it would be prudent of you to start shopping around for more affordable housing."

"This is my house we're talking about, Lou – I practically built it." Stan sat across from Lou in a booth at a local eatery, waiting for a stack of pancakes and a pile of bacon. Two coffee cups discharged strands of ethereal steam that dissipated in the dry, cool air. "There must be something that you can do – shift money around, extend the mortgage. What have I been paying for all these years?"

"You watch the news. The bubble's burst, Stan. Hit this market particularly hard." Lou sipped coffee without shifting his eyes. "Home values are falling, taxes continue to rise, and insurance rates are skyrocketing." Lou maintained a casual but professional relationship with each of his clients, remaining strictly detached in situations that pitted the bottom line of his institution against the wishes of its patrons. "It's business," Lou said, siding with the bank. The institution boasted a genial and accommodating attitude in its omnipresent advertising campaign, but when it came to actually helping people, particularly in times of economic hardship, they were merciless. "And you don't want to risk a foreclosure. Get out from under it now, while you still can."

"That wasn't really what I wanted to hear from you this morning, Lou." Stan did not bother with the glasses; he needed no validation. He pulled out the form he had been carrying around for the last 16 hours, jotted down Lou's name. He looked up in time to see the inquisitive look on his financial advisor's face. "It's nothing," Stan said. "It's just business."

****

"Such composure and optimism – it's truly admirable to see such traits in an age of rampant cynicism and negativity. Let me reward you, Stan. Let me make a proposition I believe you'll find quite agreeable."

The salesman then paused, waiting for any sign of lingering opposition. Stan leaned back in the dining room chair, folded his arms, and pursed his lips. The reality of his financial situation had, in fact, kept him up nights as his mind raced over fiscal scenarios. No matter how he juggled his budget, though, he had concluded that eventually he would have to put the house up for sale – move out of the county entirely and find some place where the cost of living would not bleed a man dry of both his savings and his hope.

"I'll take your silence as an acknowledgement of interest, then," the salesman said, sliding some paperwork across the clean, polished walnut of the dining room table. "It's all quite simple," he continued, reading from a prepared statement that had evidently been composed by wary attorneys. "We seek a specific class of transgressors and malefactors for a combination of institutional castigation and cultivation. Due to certain contractual obligations, my organization is unable to directly accumulate these subjects and therefore enlists the willing assistance of an intermediary scout, hereafter referred to as the liaison. The liaison shall accrue the names of seven subjects deemed of interest to the organization, one in each of the following categories: luxuria, gula, avaritia, acedia, ira, invidia and superbia. In return for providing these leads, the liaison will be remunerated. The amount of recompense will be no less than a $1,000,000, payable in gold bullion, to be disbursed when the liaison has fulfilled his obligations to the organization. The contract between you and the organization will be considered null and void if the liaison fails to fulfill his obligations, provides unsatisfactory information, or withholds an identity due to a conflict of interest."

Wrath
Saturday, 11:47 a.m.

It had been easy so far. His nominees had exposed themselves without much effort, without any hesitation. Stan had placed himself in civic situations – some routine, some disreputable – and the all the reprobates had emerged.

Just like upending a rotten log in the forest to uncover a host of vermin, society's underbelly swarmed with perverts and self-servers and junkies and bullies and cheats. Stan had always known this, had always been aware of the unbridled carnality and corruption plaguing the world. It had always sickened him, kept him from forming lasting relationships. His understanding of human nature had brought about his early conversion to the religion of misanthropy.

Next on the list, wrath, called to mind its most fanatical progeny, murder. At its core, though, Stan recognized something more fundamental, more universal, particularly in today's rushed environment. Wrath, Stan realized, often grew from impatience with the due process of law, be it the law of the land or the laws of the universe. That impatience bred impulsiveness, intolerance, and vigilantism.

Sitting in a traffic jam on the interstate system that dissected his town and drove adjacent property values deep into the ground, Stan found himself surrounded by routinely calm individuals overcome with rashness, aggravation, and antagonism. Delayed drivers pounded dashboards with their fists, uttered profanities, and made irreverent gestures. Some stewed quietly, their exasperation building beneath the flesh, as they stockpiled their compounding road rage in shadowy corners which would eventually erupt in a fit of anger channeled at some unsuspecting spouse or child.

Watching them through the glasses, watching them writhe and squirm in flames fanned by their own fury, Stan felt no remorse for them at all.

Stan picked the most vocal of the bunch, recorded the make and model of his car, and noted the license plate number.

****

"If you want to pay me a million bucks for a list of names," Stan said, tempering his enthusiasm, "I'm in, assuming this isn't some kind of scam. The only problem is I didn't quite catch all those fancy categories you rattled off."

"First, Stan, it's no scam. I'm not phishing for personal account information, a Social Security number, your mother's maiden name – we need none of that to proceed. There's no investment required, no buy-in to some employment scheme or pyramid deal. You just use your powers of observation to find seven candidates within the specified amount of time." The salesman signed and dated the contract from which he had just read the primary requirements of the agreement. "As far as the categories, the sheet of paper in front of you lists them in more modern terminology. Even if you're not a particularly religious man, I think you'll recognize them as the Seven Deadly Sins."

"Oh," Stan stammered, glancing at the form on the table. Like a worksheet, it listed each sin followed by a blank space which he would have to complete with the name of the sinner. In order, the sins included lust, gluttony, greed, sloth, wrath, envy and pride. "Yes," he said, scanning the document, "I get it now."

"Our prospective liaisons often ask the same questions, so I can probably clear up any uncertainties you have with a few additional bits of information. You needn't fill them out in order; a full name is preferred, but, if unavailable, a partial name or even the precise time and place where you witnessed the individual will suffice. Your name will not be published and will not be made known to those you select; your acceptance of the payment on completion of your obligations will not constitute an act of greed on your part since you were approached by our organization. However, I strongly recommend that you don't inquire about further employment." The salesman sat back in his chair, having completed his well-practiced spiel. He pushed the contract across the table toward Stan. "A few more tips: People always think *fat* for gluttony; alcohol and drug addiction is just as much a form of gluttony as excessive consumption. People always think *lazy* for sloth; apathy is a far more destructive derivation of sloth than lethargy."

Envy
Saturday, 2:45 p.m.

Stan stared at the blank spaces on the form. He could not remember exactly what time the salesman had come calling the previous afternoon. Had it been three or four in the afternoon? Everything else had fallen into place so easily, so perfectly that he wondered why something as simple as envy could cause him so much angst.

Dante described it as the "love of one's own good perverted to a desire to deprive other men of theirs," according to Stan's spur-of-the-moment Web search. The results validated his understanding of the concept without offering much inspiration. For the first time, Stan felt pressed for time and on the verge of defeat. The other sins evoked certain stereotypes that presented ample aspirants among the iniquitous, nefarious folk that populated his town. Envy, though, seemed much more abstract and ultimately less evil than its more destructive cousins.

Envy, nurtured to fruition, might make a jealous man commit an act of vandalism against a neighbor with superior material possessions; might make a covetous loner stalk the object of his desire; might sour friendships, disintegrate marriages, and impair familial relationships.

Stan glanced at a portrait of his family, taken when he was still a teenager. His younger brother, Stephen, had not spoken to him in years. He had always complained their parents favored Stan, provided Stan with more affection, and rewarded Stan's achievements with enhanced praise, exceptional attention, and excessive significance.

Stephen had been consumed by envy and had spent his lifetime using it as an excuse to veil his own mediocrity.

Stan looked at the photograph sitting on the nearby credenza, this time through the glasses. The vision he saw repulsed him. Even at that young age, the spite and resentment had begun to disfigure Stephen, transforming him into a shadow-like effigy of his older brother.

Reluctantly, Stan scribbled his name on the form.

****

"What about these?" Stan tapped the glasses sitting in the center of the table.

"I almost forgot," the salesman said, slapping his forehead with the palm of his hand. "These glasses will help you by validating your selections. Don't use them unless you're relatively certain, because the effect is quite unsettling."

Lust
Friday, 4:56 p.m.

The salesman had concluded their dealings with a firm handshake and a promise to return in 24 hours. Stan watched as he walked down the sidewalk, rounded the corner, and disappeared.

Next door, his neighbor hovered over a flowerbed. Petunias poked out from a covering of cypress mulch, swaying eagerly as she watered them with the garden hose.

He felt the glasses in his hand, felt them burning his flesh as if urging him to use them. The compulsion stirred him, even though he needed no confirmation of her sin. The whole street knew how she had cheated on her husband, gossiped still about the strangers she brought back to her place in the dead of night.

Looking at the ground, he hooked the frames over his ears. The bridge sat snugly on his nose.

When he looked up into her yard, what he saw made him gag a little. Covered head to toe in the filth of her numerous lovers, she stood naked to the world, a mass of swollen breasts and cracked lips and writhing black tentacles sprouting from a copious number of extraneous orifices.

Stan staggered back inside, pulled the glasses off his face, and let them fall to the carpeted floor. After regaining his composure, he scrawled her name on the form the salesman had provided.

****

"Well," Stan said, looking over the contract. He scratched his upper lip as he rationalized his decision. He only had to collect the names of those who had committed sins, after all. Pointing out the immorality of others seemed a passive activity at best, particularly compared to the zeal with which organized religions upheld their own ideals through ostracism, persecution, and the occasional witch hunt. "Where do I sign?"

"At the very bottom," the salesman said, smiling. "But first, the only stipulation we have not discussed is the time frame. Each liaison generally requires a different amount of time to fulfill the obligations. How long do you believe it will take you to come up with seven names?"

"I don't know, shouldn't take too long," Stan said, boasting. Considering the number of sins reported daily on the local news and in the newspapers, considering the fact that he could pin a sin on two or three of his neighbors, his confidence redoubled. "What's the normal time?"

"It averages, anywhere from a week to a few months," the salesman said. "Had one fellow recently who managed to get all of his names within 48 hours."

"I could do it in less, I bet," Stan said, his competitiveness getting the best of him. "Let's say 24 hours."

"Very well," the salesman said, watching as Stan signed the contract. "I'll see you in 24 hours, Stan."

Pride
Saturday, 3:35 p.m.

Stan shambled out of the bathroom, the preternatural glasses abandoned on the terrazzo floor near the edge of the bathtub, at least one lens shattered. The salesman's insistent knocking had finally stirred him from his humiliation, reaching some part of him that still believed a reprieve might be possible.

"Time's up, Stan," the salesman said, barging inside the moment the door opened. His presumption and audacity would have solicited a stern reprimand from Stan on any other day; but, today, he found himself incapable of putting up a struggle. "Let's see how well you've done. Where is your list?"

"There," Stan said, pointing to the coffee table in the living room. The pen with which he had added his brother's name to the list sat dormant alongside the piece of paper. "I'm not finished," he said, the words spilling awkwardly over his lips. "I've only been able to get six names …"

"Oh, come now, Stan," the salesman said, "I'm sure you've got the seventh name … I'll be happy to give you a moment to add it to the list."

"No, I … there's nothing more," Stan said, sounding somewhat nervous. "Only six, that's all."

"Strange," the salesman said, reviewing the names on the list. "The only one missing is pride. Are you sure you haven't managed to find anyone that might fit that category?"

"I couldn't," Stan stammered.

"Well, this is unfortunate," the salesman said. "Not only have you failed to meet your obligations by not finding seven candidates, you have also withheld a name due to a conflict of interest."

"What are you talking about?"

"Stan, your glasses transmitted every sin you beheld, every soul you scrutinized." The salesman eased himself onto the sofa, his fingers toying with the drapery covering the front window. "I watched as you judged them all, watched as you ferreted them out like the parasites they are. You lived up to your potential … until you stumbled over your own pride. I know what you saw in the mirror."

"What will happen to me now?" Stan had never realized just how discriminatory he had become. What had been academic dignity in school had become arrogance in adulthood. What had been attention to personal fitness in his youth had become narcissism in middle age. What had been a predisposition for virtue and decency had become unwarranted righteousness and elitism. "Will you add my name to the list?"

"Of course not, Stan – I can't do that." The salesman picked up the form and scanned it, line for line. He appeared impressed with the candidates Stan had selected. "Shame, really – some very good contenders here. We've had our eye on some of them for some time. Some, on the other hand, are new to us." He wadded up the paper, set it back on the coffee table and scowled as it erupted in a small ball of flame. "Look, I'm not the devil, Stan. It's not my job to track these people down and haul them off to hell – not yet, anyway. So relax."

"That's it?"

"That's it. I'm sorry about the money, I know you could have used it." The salesman stood, showed himself to the door. "Good luck," he said as he left. He paused in the doorway, looked over his shoulder. "And Stan: You might want to try to keep yourself off anyone else's list in the future."

The End

Vampire Wine by Marge Simon

Now is the time for Vampire wine,
sweet as Madeira, but not from the vine,
it's always the time for Vampire wine.

The curse that in her cup abides
will beg a taste divine,
eternal life within each sip
beware her vampire wine!

Now is the time for Vampire wine,
sweet as Madeira, but not from the vine,
it's always the time for Vampire wine.

She drinks to you only with her eyes
her allure has you in her thrall,
this exquisite vision is merely a guise,
her kiss the deadliest of all.

Now is the time for Vampire wine,
sweet as Madeira, but not from the vine,
it's always the time for Vampire wine.

Phantom
by
Christopher T. Dabrowski

When the light went off, Adam ran to his bedroom to hide under the covers as fast as he could. When his parents went out to see some friends, he was happy. He could finally taste the feeling of having the whole apartment to himself. This was going to be fun!

Downstairs, in the dining room, he installed military bases. On the bookcases that turned into mountains, there were patrols of a few plastic soldiers at the books; and behind the table, there were some tanks. This time, it was going to be total war.

"The first home war." He giggled.

He was just heading to the next toy – after all, he still had to do something in the parents' bedroom and the attic – when the lights went off. Surprised by sudden darkness, he froze still, nailed with an icy sting of panic. A moment later, he was speeding, as fast as his legs would allow, to his bed. Hidden with the covers up to the tip of his nose, he tried to hold his breath so that nothing could hear him. His heart pounded as if it wanted to escape from his skinny chest. He hid his head under the covers and turned himself into a tiny, scared ball. Apart from the thudding sound of his heart and intermittent breaths, he couldn't hear anything. He just wanted his parents to come back as soon as possible; he was afraid of what could lurk in the never-ending darkness of the old house.

After a few minutes, he got a bit calmer. The thick, warm blankets gave him an elusive sense of safety. He hoped that whatever evil was roaming his house wouldn't be able to find him.

He had no idea what could be going on outside. There could be a vicious ghost at the window staring with its dead eyes at his hideout. Maybe *something* dark came out from the wardrobe and sniffed with a ferocious look in its red eyes because it could smell a scared little boy. Many terrible things could be under the bed, but here, under the blanket, he was safe. It was irrational, but that was how he felt.

Over time, Adam started to get warm. What's more, the longer he lay without any move, the more he felt something disturbing him. He didn't like that feeling. All he needed was light – just that – and he could forget his discomfort; he could play undisturbed. And generally, how could he be sure that the evil creatures wouldn't figure out that he was hiding in his bed?

He felt threatened. Fear surrounded him with its paralyzing tentacles.

The moonlight did its best to sneak through the dense curtains and lighten the interior of the bedroom. Behind the window, wind hissed. A moment later, the sound of rain knocking on the windowpane was added. The boy finally gathered all his courage to make a small slit between the cover and the bed; now, he could breathe in some fresh air.

He was scared that a spooky tentacle would appear from under the bed and pull him into where it came from. He was forcing his eyes, trying to see any potential danger. After a few seconds, his eyes adjusted to the darkness around him. Adam stuck his head out from under the blanket, and he saw several viciously sparkling eyes. His heart froze, touched by fear, but a moment later, he recalled that a few days before, he had put a collection of teddy bears on the shelves. It was their glassy eyes that were shining evilly.

Oh, you ungrateful bears! Adam sighed with relief. He looked deeper into the room; there was a big black shape, but luckily, he remembered it was just a wardrobe.

Just a wardrobe, but there could be *something* inside it...

Clouds hid the moon and it got darker. The rain drummed stronger and louder. The boy wondered if he should risk going out of the bed. After all, there was a decorative candle on the cupboard. He would feel a lot better if he could light it and make sure he was safe.

Safe? You must be kidding, fool! An evil voice laughed in his head. *You'd rather have the chance to look at a bloodthirsty creature that would jump on you from a dark corner!*

"Shut up!" Adam hissed under his nose and jumped from the bed. He wanted to get over all that nightmare.

Suddenly, amazing light flooded the room, blinding the boy for a second. He screamed, terrified, and almost at the same time, he heard a great thump. Adam threw himself towards the bed. He jumped under the blanket, banging his leg against something hard.

"It's just thunder, just thunder, just a thunder," he whispered, trembling, trying to convince himself that nothing wrong was going on, that he was safe. When he calmed down a bit, he realized his pajama pants were cold and wet.

"Oh, no, I pissed!" he moaned.

He jumped from the bed not to wet the covers – he hoped to cover the traces before his parents would return – and he felt a painful hit in his leg. He bit his teeth and tumbled to the cupboard. This unpleasant adventure made him forget about the suffocating fear for a while.

Yellowish candlelight made the vicious darkness less evil, offering a moment of safety. The pajama pants were wet from urine, that was sure, and there was a purple bruise on the leg. Luckily, the bed was untouched. The sheet and the blanket were only slightly spotted.

No one will know, Adam thought, relieved.

The only drawback of this situation was that now he would have to wash himself and the pajamas. So he was about to face going through the darkness, climbing to the attic where the bathroom was located. Of course, there was another one on the first floor, but it was being rebuilt.

He wasn't happy about the journey, but he knew he had no other choice.

Another lightning stroke in the neighborhood.

The faster, the better. He'd check what he had to check – whether there were any foul creatures in the room. He would take clean pajamas from the cupboard and then go upstairs.

He knelt and peeked. Nothing under the bed. He tiptoed to the old wardrobe; he was most afraid of what could hide in its large wooden body. He pressed his ear against the door, but he heard nothing – purely perfect silence inside.

Maybe it is lurking? Adam bit his lip, uncertain. Just one fast move, no matter what happens! Just one quick move, and it would turn out that Mum was again right – nothing in there.

Right, right, just one fast move, and sticky tentacles will shoot from the darkness. They will slither around your wrists and pull you into another dimension, a harsh voice whispered into his ear. *You know, a lot of children disappear in unknown circumstances. Do you want to be next? Okay, just go on.*

"Shut up! Just shut up!" Adam commanded with a calm, orderly tone, knowing that he must overcome the fear. After all, he was almost ten, a man; he simply had to stop being scared!

With one fast move, he opened the wardrobe. The door objected with a loud groan. He froze, terrified...

For a moment, inside the vast furniture, he could see *something* –that made him tremble— *something*!

He laughed in a high voice. It was just an old, cuddled blanket, just a stupid blanket, but for one horrible moment, he thought he saw a brown demon body.

"See, nothing to be afraid of," He comforted himself, as he still couldn't believe his eyes.

Relieved, he closed the door and froze. With the corner of his eye, he caught a glimpse of movement.

Well, the monster was cleverer than you expected, the internal critic mocked him. *He took you from behind, you loser. Now what?*

But nothing happened, and Adam decided it must have been his imagination. The room was empty. Not to waste any more time, the boy took clean pajamas from the drawer and went towards the door.

"Okay, here I go." He pressed the doorknob and went out of the room.

In the distance, eyes shone in the darkness. Their owner moved a few meters and ... meowed miserably. Of course, Donald! Adam still didn't get used to the fact that they owned a cat. New (old) house. New family member – brownish cat walking its own paths, and only sometimes paying a bit of his attention to the new owners.

Cats don't have masters; cats have servants, as someone once said.

New town, new school – far too many new things. Eh, if anything was up to Adam ... but no one ever listened to him; such fate...

He closed the door and went towards the stairs that led to the attic.

From the portraits on the walls, eyes of someone else's descendants shone with oil paints. The boy wondered why his parents didn't take down those disgusting paintings. They were all ugly faces! Trying not to pay attention to the numb, dead observers, he rushed upstairs; each step was accompanied by an unpleasant squeak.

Luckily, the bathroom door was next to the stairs. He sighed with relief, realizing that all this stress would be over in a flash. Laundry, washing, and back to bed – to sleep. He had lost his interest in playing.

Sparkling candlelight reflected from the wall plates, making the bathroom shine with vibrating reflections. It looked like the interior of a tomb filled with treasures. Adam set the candle on the edge of the bathtub, took off his wet pants, then reached for the candle again. He went to the sink. When he looked in the mirror, an icy sting of fear bit his heart.

What he saw made his eyes almost leave their sockets. Now it was not only the pants he had to wash. He also had to clean the floor, but at this very moment, he couldn't think about it. All his universe shrank to what he could see in the mirror. He was breathing spasmodically, wheezing like an asthmatic patient.

His body trembled; his forehead sparkled with sweat. He felt weak. Adam knew that a moment more, and he would faint. He bit his lip as hard as he could, almost until he felt blood. For a moment, he pushed the overwhelming weakness aside, just enough to stand still and not fall. He wanted to run as fast and far as he could; he couldn't believe that what he saw was true. Despite his paralyzing fear, with extreme effort, he made himself touch his face.

Yes, his face was unchanged. He was still himself – a small, scared boy!

But why did the mirror show a half-naked, toothless old man with hanging, wrinkled skin? The phantom looked at him with its bloody, bruised eyes with yellowish whites.

The boy felt increasingly dizzy. The stiff hand could not hold the candle anymore. Darkness waded in, enabling him to escape, blindly, as far from the mirror as possible...

****

Old age has its advantages, but it also has drawbacks.

Unfortunately, the latter are significantly more numerous.

Of course, life gets easier; you don't have to work. You can taste each day like a ripe fruit. You see many details that were previously overlooked. Due to a lack of time to take a closer look, the details flew by in the background of life, lost forever. But these details are the spice that gives your life specificity, taste, making it richer with a deeper dimension.

The old man could appreciate all this; he only regretted that it took him so long to understand this truth.

Unfortunately, there are also sad moments, and they get increasingly frequent. In old age, you become disabled. You have problems controlling your physiological processes – simply speaking, pissing in his pants was nothing new to him. He got used to it and accepted it. After all, there had to be something on both sides of the scales of life.

These problems were not the worst ones. Even pain or trembling hands – sometimes this was so intensive that anything he touched landed on the floor within split seconds – nothing was as scary as the fact that he increasingly often forgot what happened.

In the beginning, only from time to time, he had forgotten where he had put things. Then it happened more often. Events and memories got all mixed up. Then he started having problems with recognizing people and places, which made him avoid leaving his home. Then he felt like an invalid.

After a few years, the disease progressed so badly that sometimes he didn't know what he did a moment earlier, where he was, but the worst thing was that sometimes he didn't even know... *who* he was.

Oldness, like a mean vampire, was sucking memory and clearness of thinking out of his mind.

Now it happened again. This time he remembered who he was, but he couldn't realize why he was standing next to a mirror with a candle in his hand.

He came closer and ... saw a little boy – himself from over eighty years ago.

A tear appeared in Adam's eye.

"That was long ago!" He sighed.

He wasn't surprised by what he saw in the mirror; people don't get surprised easily at this age. He decided that he was either sleeping or it was another phantom, a creation of an old, worn brain. The only feeling he had now was a deep, touching emotion. In his mind's eye, he saw long-forgotten scenes from his childhood, crazy times when he could do all kinds of exciting things and no one had any problem with it.

So many years have passed in a flash; eighty-eight or maybe eighty-nine – he sometimes forgot even his own age, but what difference did it make?

None!

"Well, what comes around, goes around," he whispered and blew off the flame.

Darkness surrounded him, and that was okay with him.

The End

An award-winning short film was made in England based on this story: https://www.facebook.com/phantomfilm. Link to trailer: https://www.youtube.com/watch?v=cJQBOFLE4N0

Mind and Body by Sravani Singampalli

They say that his blood stinks.
His red blood cells are rotting away
Because of his misdeeds and
White blood cells have refused
To fight for him.
He knows that he was wrong that day.
He knew the repercussions.
Today those poor people have lost homes
Their children can't go to school
Just because of him.
Now, their hunger has cursed him.
His body is slowly deteriorating.
He asks for forgiveness
But some leaves
Have already wilted.

A Hunters Regret by Matthew Wilson

Werewolf pelt for sale
willing to swap for bane antidote.
speedy trade preferred.

Haiku III by Denny E. Marshall

didn't donate blood
full moon midnight appointment
rather suspicious

Imram by Lee Clark Zumpe

To an island set upon four pillars
Where time passes unnoticed.
No grieving, no winter, no want;
And home falls beneath the sediment
Of centuries.

To an island of the Otherworld
Where birds in harmony call.
No grave, no famine, no fear;
Yet home calls the wistful traveler
To return.

Crepuscular Fiend
by
Rajeev Bhargava

The huge red and black brick mansion stood in all its grandeur, in the remote countryside, amidst the cold bare trees, a relic from a time long ago. However, it had a mysterious past, so was considered haunted. Rumors had spread that its *occupant* was something so horrid that nobody dared set foot inside. In fact, anyone who even glanced at it would suffer a bad fate in their lifetime.

"Very impressive!" quipped the attractive young lady tourist in her mid-twenties as she stopped across the winding pathway to catch sight of it.

"*Don't look at it, Jelena!*" called out her partner, a lanky, spectacled man in his late thirties. She giggled and placed her hands into his.

"Oh, don't be so jumpy, Andy. I'm going inside. Come on!"

In a last desperate bid, he clasped her hands and pleaded with her. "*Please.* If you care about my feelings, then let's move on. Besides, I'm sure there are other places where we can lodge."

"You must be joking. My feet have blisters after walking for hours. Besides, this was all your idea, to find a nice spot where you can pick up ideas for your new book. Now, are you coming or not?"

"Well, don't say I didn't warn you. We both know about the rumors that revolve around that creepy place."

"Creepy? Just look at it. It's so beautiful and majestic. I always dreamed of living in a place like that."

This time, Jelena did not wait for his response and made her way forward.

Andy shrugged, then followed her. They continued up the narrow granite trail leading to the main door.

"There. That wasn't so difficult now, was it, Andy, hmm?" She poked him in his abdomen with her left hand and giggled.

"Ouch. Hah, hah, very amusing."

The door was well polished with thick green and black paint.

"One thing is for certain, Andy. The occupant is very particular about maintaining the beauty of this place. Now let's go in."

"No, wait!" Andy protested. "We can't just walk in."

"Honestly, did you *really* think I was going to do that? Duh!" She searched for the doorbell or a doorknob. There wasn't any.

"How odd!" said Jelena. The heavy door partially opened. There was just enough space for them to enter. Once inside, the door slammed shut behind them, and there was the sound of a heavy bolt.

"Oh, no, you've really done it. We're locked in. See, I did warn you!" Andy banged on the door. "Help! Help!!"

Jelena slapped him hard on his left cheek.

"Stop it at once! You're such a big baby. Honestly! I know it was my idea, so I take full responsibility to get us both out of here. Just trust me, all right?"

He nodded.

"Good. Now take a deep breath and follow me."

The room was somber, murky, and unlit. Everything appeared blurred and misty, so much so that neither of them could make out anything clearly.

Something brushed against Andy and he jumped.

"Aaahhh!!!"

"What is it now?" yelled Jelena with a frown. "Just stop it, or I'll go crazy."

"Not you, Jelena. I'll go crazy! I'm not going a step further. Let's get out of this place."

Just then, a melodious sound filled the air. It seemed to come from above. Jelena held Andy's right hand and proceeded up the spiral staircase.

"Err, aren't we supposed to be going towards the main door, Jelena?"

Jelena ignored Andy's protest and continued up the flight of stairs until a long shadow fell across the top step. Someone was approaching.

"There's still time. Quickly, let's hide!" said Andy nervously. He tugged himself free from Jelena, ran back downstairs, and vanished in the dusk.

"Jelena Crepson! Long time no see!"

"Aunt Wertila! What a pleasant surprise."

A tall, slim, and attractive lady with long scarlet hair stood at the top of the stairs and beckoned to Jelena.

Jelena smiled and followed her aunt along the corridor. Along the way, the darkness turned to an illuminating yellow light. In a few seconds, the color changed to orange, then blue, yellow, and green.

"Oh, that's beautiful!" cried Jelena.

Aunt Wertila smiled. "The colors will keep changing. They're fluorescent."

"Excuse me, Aunty, I'll be right back." Jelena turned back to the stairs and called out at the top of her voice, "Andy! Come on up and meet Aunt Wertila. Andy!"

There was no reply.

"Wait, let me summon him," Aunt Wertila said.

She snapped her left hand, and in an instant, Andy appeared before them, from out of the air. He looked around, confused.

"How did you do *that*, Aunty?" asked Jelena.

"I've had this gift since birth. I never told a soul." She tapped her nose and smiled. "Come on. I'll show you both to your rooms."

"See, Jelena. I told you. Woof, woof, woof!" Andy held his throat and turned to her, wide-eyed. "Woof … woof."

"Leave us in peace, you bad brat!" stormed Aunt Wertila.

She grabbed Andy's left ear and marched him to a side room. After pushing him inside, she bolted the door. She then smiled, straightened her crimson gown, and walked back to Jelena, who watched, wide-eyed.

"Was that really necessary, Aunt Wertila?"

"Oh, the effect will wear off in a couple of hours. Now follow me. I'm dying to show you something."

They soon arrived at a large green door with a purple skull on it. Aunt Wertila opened the door. As she stepped into the room, she turned invisible.

"Come and find me!" she called out to Jelena.

Jelena stepped inside, then found she could not move. Her feet were literally glued to the carpet. She looked around and shouted, "That's not funny, Aunty. Please release me."

There was no reply. Just pin-drop silence. Jelena began to sob and repent her adamant decision to go inside.

"I'm sorry, Andy. I should have listened to you."

Just then, a loud thud sounded from the corridor.

"Andy? Andy, I'm in here!"

A large shadow fell across the floor, followed by heavy breathing. In a desperate bid to free herself, Jelena squeezed her eyes shut, then crouched to the floor and heaved upwards with all her force.

"Aaahhhh!!" Her body jetted into the air and fell sideways on the hard concrete floor. Darkness followed…

When her eyes opened, Jelena found Andy kneeling over her with a look of concern.

"Andy. You're all right. What happened?"

"No, don't get up, Jelena. Stay as you are."

"Why?" She looked around to observe her surroundings.

"We're in the basement; that's where your beloved aunt locked me. I used my canine strength to knock the blasted door down." As he spoke, saliva dribbled from his mouth onto the floor.

"Ewww!! Jelena grimaced as some landed on her legs. She also noted he had paws. "Andy! Where are your feet!?"

"Oh, wake up, Jelena, for goodness sake. Woof, woof!" He coughed. A moment's silence, then she giggled.

"Andy, you've not only changed into a hybrid, but you've also become more aggressive."

"I know." Andy lowered his head. "I can't help it. Your Aunt Wertila put a spell on me. Woof, woof."

Jelena thought hard. "If we make an escape, you'll remain this way for good. There's only one way out. We will have to give ourselves in to Aunt Wertila and plead with her."

"I somehow don't think that's a very good idea, Jelena."

The basement door flung open.

"There you are!! shouted out Aunt Wertila. "Come on out, both of you. Now!"

Andy and Jelena made their way out the basement and followed Aunt Wertila into a chamber room. But as her dress brushed against the door, it caught around its sharp edges and tore off to reveal something that left them aghast.

Andy covered Jelena's eyes."

The lower half of Aunt Wertila's body was that of a snake, and her skin was made up of scales and speckles.

"What is it, Andy?" cried out Jelena, wide-eyed.

"I don't know, Jelena, but it's definitely not human."

"Correct!" A pained voice said from behind them. "It's an echidna."

A slimy hand fell across Jelena's right shoulder. She screamed.

"Ruff, ruff!" called out Andy, then turned to give Aunt Wertila a vicious bite.

"No, please don't. Like yourselves, I, too, was locked inside here for the past twenty years. This was my home until *that* monstrosity found a way in and has been feeding off my flesh as the prime source of nourishment. Now, she's going to get you, too!"

"Quickly, let's get out of here, Jelena," Andy said. "Or else that monstrosity is going to chew us up alive!"

Andy held her hand tightly and made a run for the main door. The echidna hissed and slid forwards but was held back by her tail.

"Let go of me, you fool."

"No. I can't let you harm them," said Aunt Wertila. "This is my home, and you kept me as a pet zombie, but … there's still some human consciousness left in me."

"That's it." The echidna's eyes turned a deep green, and she opened her mouth to reveal razor-sharp teeth.

"Goodbye!" Then she leaned forwards and bit into her chest, pulling out her heart. She chomped at it and swallowed. Blood oozed and dribbled down her lips onto the floor.

In the meantime, Jelena had managed to find a large candlestand on the mantle and bashed open the bolted door. They were free.

But little did they realize a small group of echidnas was waiting to feast on them amidst the tall, dark trees that surrounded the outskirts of the manor…

The End

About the Contributors

Linda Barrett:

Ms. Barrett has been writing all her life. She wrote her first book at the age of eight. It's still in the McKinley Elementary school library. She was published in the *Huntingdon Junior Library* literary magazine by age thirteen. She's won three awards with the Montgomery County Community College Writer's contest. "Mr. Cat's Revenge" won third place in the 2014 MCCC contest. Ms. Barrett lives with her 84 years young mother in Abington in the same house for 50 years."

Rajeev Bhargava:

Rajeev lives in Harrow with his parents and five Chihuahuas. He has been writing since the age of twelve but had his first work published in 1990. Since then he's been writing stories, poems and articles for the small press as well as mainstream. His ambition is to be a freelance writer.

Gerald Browning:

Gerald Browning is a husband, father, writer, and martial artist who teaches English and Literature for Muskegon Community College and Grand Valley State University. He enjoys reading philosophy and history. He cross-trains in multiple martial arts and has published in other popular culture books, and is an avid writer of horror fiction. His first horror novel is titled, *Demon in My Head*.

Margaret L. Carter:

Reading *Dracula* at the age of twelve ignited Margaret L. Carter's interest in a wide range of speculative fiction and inspired her to become a writer. Vampires, however, have always remained close to her heart. Her work on vampirism in literature includes *Dracula: The Vampire and the Critics, The Vampire in Literature, A Critical Bibliography*, and *Different Blood: The Vampire as Alien*. She holds a PhD in English from the University of California (Irvine), and her dissertation contained a chapter on *Dracula*. In fiction, she has written horror, fantasy, and paranormal romance. Recent publications include *Crimson Dreams* (vampire romance), *Demon's Fall* (paranormal romance novella), *Heart's Desires and Dark Embraces* (story collection, fantasy and paranormal romance), and *Legacy of Magic* (sword and sorcery, in collaboration with her husband, Leslie Roy Carter). Her short stories have been published in anthologies such as the "Sword and Sorceress" and "Darkover" volumes, among others. "A Walk in the Mountains," co-written with her husband, appeared in the 2016 anthology *Realms of Darkover*. A sequel, "Believing," was included in *Masques of Darkover* (2017). Margaret's solo humorous ghost story, "Haunted Book Nook," appeared in the anthology *Sword and Sorceress* 33 (2018). She and her husband, a retired naval officer, live in Maryland and have four sons, several grandchildren and great-grandchildren, a St. Bernard, and two cats.

Mariel Milan Cruz:

Mariel was born and raised in Puerto Rico. She's been living in a small town of Missouri for 13 years. At 38 years old, she's a massage therapist and a mother of four children. She's currently staying at home full time taking care of two-year-old boy and girl twins.

Christopher T. Dabrowski:

Christopher has had numerous books published in the USA and Poland. His USA works include: *Anomaly* and *Escape*, both published by the Royal Hawaiian Press. Books published in Poland include *Anima Vilis* (Initium), *Grobbing* (Novae Res), *Deathbirth and other Stories* (Agharta & Amoryka), *Orgazmokalipsa* (Alternatywne publishing house), *Anomalia* (Forma publishing house), and *Ucieczka* (2017 - Dom Horroru publishing house). Monika Olasek provided the English translation for his *Night to Dawn* stories.

Sandy DeLuca:

Sandy has written five novels; *Settling in Nazareth* (she painted the cover art), *Descent, Manhattan Grimoire, From Ashes,* and *Requiem for the Dead.* Her poetry chapbook, *Burial Plot in Sagittarius* (also created cover art and illustrations), was nominated for the BRAM STOKER award in 2001. Her art has been exhibited in galleries, hair salons, book stores and online venues. She has also painted covers and contributed interior illustrations for various numerous small press venues.

Richard H. Fay:

Formerly a laboratory technician-turned-home-educator, Richard H. Fay now spends his days writing and creating art. He often draws inspiration from history, myth, folklore, and legend. Many of the fruits of Richard's creative labors have appeared in various e-zines, print magazines, and anthologies. Merchandise featuring Richard's artworks and designs sells internationally through several online print-on-demand stores.

Chris Friend:

Chris has published his art in small press horror magazines for nearly 25 years. His surreal horror images have been featured in *Stygian Articles, Realm of the Vampire, Deathrealm, Black Petals,* and *Space and Time.* He draws his inspiration from Harry Clarke, H. R. Giger, and the horror comics of the 70s such as the Tomb of Dracula her and the Hammer Studios Frankenstein films. Chris friend can be reached at Mars_art_13@yahoo.com. Chris friend can be reached at Mars_art_13@yahoo.com.

To sample his illustrations, go to http://chris.michaelherring.net and http://www.moonlit-path.com/art-2-13-06.htm.

Ken Goldman:

Ken Goldman, former Philadelphia teacher of English and Film Studies, is an Active member of the Horror Writers Association. He has homes on the Main Line in Pennsylvania and at the Jersey shore. His stories have appeared in over 930 independent press publications in the U.S., Canada, the UK, and Australia with over thirty due for publication in 2020. Since 1993, Ken's tales have received seven honorable mentions in The Year's Best Fantasy & Horror. He has written six books: three anthologies of short stories, *You Had Me at ARRGH!!* (Sam's Dot Publishers), *Donny Doesn't Live Here Anymore* (A/A Productions) and *Star-Crossed* (Vampires 2); and a novella, *Desiree,* (Damnation Books). His first novel *Of a Feather* (Horrific Tales Publishing) was released in January 2014. *Sinkhole,* his second novel, was published by Bloodshot Books August 2017.

Todd Hanks:

The creative writing of Todd Hanks has been seen in publications such as Asimov's Science Fiction Magazine and the Kansas City Star newspaper.

Hal Kempka:

Hal's stories have been published in numerous magazines and ezines including *Night to Dawn, Blood Moon Rising, Black Petals, Inner Sins, Sanitarium, Yellow Mama,* and *Microhorror.* His horror short fiction anthologies, *Blue Plate Special* and *Discarded Treasures,* are currently available on Amazon Kindle, Barnes and Noble, and Smashwords, among others. *Discarded Treasures* is available in both paperback and e-book. Other anthologies including his stories are Pill Hill Press: *Zombie Art Inspired Short Stories, Blood Bound Books: Seasons in the Abyss,* and Post Mortem Press: *Shadowplay.*

Tom Johnson:

Tom, a Vietnam veteran with twenty years in the military police (L.E.), has enjoyed literary success as a science fiction novelist with his action adventures in the Jurassic Period of Earth's predawn. He has created short story SF characters like Captain Danger of the *Space Rangers* and the galactic master thief, *The Forever Man* as futuristic space opera adventure. His many costumed crime fighters include two of his own creations, such as *The Black Ghost* and *The Masked Avenger,* as well as a western masked hero of the plains called *The Nightwind.* He has upcoming stories of *Ki-Gor the Jungle Lord,* and Greek heroes like Hercules and Atalanta. For the latest information on Tom and his writing, check out his websites:

http://www15.brinkster.com/jur1/index.html
www.geocities.com/fadingshadows1/index.html.

Rod Marsden:

Rod Marsden hails from Sydney, Australia. He has three degrees related to writing and history. His stories have been published in Australia, England, Russia, the USA and now Canada. He has work in the American anthology *Cats Do it Better,* the American steam punkanthology *Break Time* and in the Canadian anthology *Morbid Metamorphosis.* Many of his short stories have been published in *Night to Dawn* magazine. His books include *Undead Reb Down Under and Other Vampire Stories, Disco Evil: Dead Man's Stand, Ghost Dance,* and *Desk Job* (his salute to Lewis Carroll). *Cold Water Conscience* is his venture into Crime/Horror. His short play, *Zombie Vision,* was well received at Cronulla Arts Theatre. His play *Hyde and Seek* was even better received. Rod has a fondness for Cronulla and the Wollongong area but an abiding love for the more northern Clarence River region of his home state of New South Wales.

Denny E. Marshall:

Denny E. Marshall has had art, poetry, and fiction published. Some recent credits include interior art in *Midnight Echo #14* Dec. 2019, cover art for *Society Of Misfit Stories* Feb. 2020, and poetry in *Space & Time Magazine #134* Fall 2019. This year his website is celebrating 20 years on the web. Also in 2020 his artwork is for sale for the first time. It is available on Zazzle as posters coffee cups, puzzles, mouse pads, etc. The link is on his website. (Click on top left drawing.) See more at www.dennymarshall.com.

Elizabeth Hattie Pierce-Collins:

Elizabeth first learned art and drawing from her mother. From there, she was self-taught until she was able to attend art school. She loves drawing the human figure and never stops studying the human body in motion. Her illustrations have appeared in *Night to Dawn* magazine and *The Spider's Web* (a novel). These have drawn positive attention from the readers. Elizabeth hopes to appear in more magazines and books in the future. For more information, contact Elizabeth at wackyursalinan45@aol.com.

Marc Shapiro:

Marc has been a busy beaver. His story *Let Me Take You Down* was printed in book form in the Short Sharp Shocks imprint of Demain Publishing on December 31. Upcoming from Demain is his debut poetry collection *Existential Jibber Jabber.* Already out: his unauthorized biography of Keanu Reeves entitled *Keanu Reeves Excellent Adventure* (Riverdale Avenue Books) and the shortest story he's ever written, four sentences under 100 words, on the website Warp 10 Lit. Marc Shapiro has a very patient and understanding wife.

Marge Simon:

Marge Simon's works appear in publications such as DailySF Magazine, Pedestal, Dreams& Nightmares. She edits a column for the HWA Newsletter, "Blood & Spades: Poets of the Dark Side," and serves as Chair of the Board of Trustees. She won the Strange Horizons Readers Choice Award, 2010, and the SFPA's Dwarf Stars Award, 2012. She has won three Bram Stoker Awards ® for Superior Work in Poetry, two first place Rhysling Awards and the Grand Master Award from the SF Poetry Association, 2015. In addition to her poetry, she has published two prose collections: *Christina's World,* Sam's Dot Publications, 2008 and *Like Birds in the Rain,* Sam's Dot, 2007. Her poems appear in *Qualia Nous* (Written Backwards), *The Dark Phantastique* (Jasunni Productions), Spectral Realms anthologies by S.T. Joshi, and more poems will appear in *Chiral Mad 3* and *Scary Out There,* a HWA/ Simon & Schuster Y/A collection, 2015. www.margesimon.com

Sravani Singampalli:

Sravani Singampalli is a published writer, poet and artist from India. Her works are published or forthcoming in many online and print journals and magazines. She is the winner of the Fiesta Love Poetry Competition 2018 and the 1st Submittable - Centric Poetry Contest. She was also one of the finalists for the Poetry Matters Poetry Contest and has won many prizes for her poetry. Her works were nominated for the Best of the net Anthology award by the Scarlet Leaf Review and the Spirit Fire Review.

Matthew Wilson:

    Matthew Wilson has had over 150 appearances in such places as *Horror Zine, Star*Line, Spellbound, Illumen, Apokrupha Press, Gaslight Press, Sorcerers Signal* and many more. He is currently editing his first novel and can be contacted on twitter @matthew94544267.

Lee Clark Zumpe:

    Lee Clark Zumpe has been writing and publishing horror, dark fantasy and speculative fiction since the late 1990s. His short stories and poetry have appeared in a variety of publications such as *Weird Tales, Space and Time* and *Dark Wisdom;* and in anthologies such as *Dark Horizons, Best New Zombie Tales Vol. 3, Dread Shadows in Paradise, Heroes of Red Hook* and *World War Cthulhu.* His work has earned several honorable mentions in *The Year's Best Fantasy and Horror* collections.

    An entertainment columnist with Tampa Bay Newspapers, Lee has penned hundreds of film, theater and book reviews and has interviewed novelists as well as music industry icons such as Paddy Moloney of The Chieftains and Alan Parsons. His work for TBN has been recognized repeatedly by the Florida Press Association, including a first-place award for criticism in the 2013 Better Weekly Newspaper Contest.